MURDER BY DESIGN

J.P. BOWIE

Murder by Design
ISBN # 978-1-83943-863-9

Interior text design by Claire Siemaszkiewicz
Pride Publishing

Published in 2020 by Pride Publishing, United Kingdom.

Pride Publishing is an imprint of Totally Entwined Group Limited.

MURDER BY DESIGN

Dedication

Thanks once more to Claire at Pride Publishing and to Rebecca my super editor for their continued help and encouragement. Also to Phil who has stuck by me for 24 years and never complained…well, that's my story and I'm sticking with it.

Prologue

The tall Hispanic man sighed as he regarded the petite woman glaring back at him, her eyes blazing with rage.

"You dare to deny me what is rightfully mine?" she screamed at him.

"I have told you, Golden Finance is going through a rough patch. There is not enough money to expand your business."

"*Mentiroso!*" she spat. "You lie! Stop wining and dining your *putas* and there will be plenty money. You think I don't know what you are doing behind my back?"

He clenched his hands into fists, trying to control the anger that built inside him, threatening to explode at any moment. He took a step backward from her in case he actually did what he longed to do. This bitch had made his life a living hell for the past two years with her constant carping, complaining and threats of exposing him as an adulterer. He had asked her for a divorce, but she'd refused, suddenly following Catholic doctrine after ignoring the Church for years.

"And don't even dare broach the subject of divorce again," she continued to rant at him. "We are married until death do us part, and don't forget it. Now, I want that money so you'd better find a way of getting it. *Entiéndeme?"*

"I understand only too well." He swung away from her, the blood pounding in his temples, his rage mounting with every spiteful word that spewed from her mouth.

"Don't you dare walk away from me. *Bastardo!*" She grabbed his arm and smacked him hard across the face.

For a moment he almost lost control. Almost reached out to take her by the throat and throttle the life out of her…stop her hateful rhetoric forever. Instead he turned away and strode toward the door, slamming it behind him, his wife's shrieking not at all dampened by the barrier of wood and glass. He paused to take a few deep breaths.

A woman stood in the hall, regarding him with sympathy, but he could not bring himself to have an even halfway normal conversation at that moment. He nodded as he passed her, feeling her eyes on his back while he made for the elevator. When the doors opened he glanced at her and said, "Later."

Chapter One

Los Angeles, California

Every time Sam Walker woke up with a hangover to end all hangovers, he vowed never to go on another bender again. Okay, so last night had been a kind of celebration and the guys from the precinct had more or less forced him into joining them in their favorite bar…but still, was this awful freaking headache and queasy stomach worth it? Carefully, he eased himself out of bed and headed with unsteady steps to the bathroom.

Staring at himself in his bathroom mirror, he groaned. *Jeez…a face only a mother could love, or so the saying goes.* Well, maybe not his mother. She hadn't loved anything about him for a long time. It wasn't the handsomest mug at the best of times, in his opinion. His jaw was too square and that stupid cleft in his chin made it hard to shave without a deal of careful blade maneuvering. He sighed and pulled down his lower eyelid, shuddering at the red that was practically overwhelming the blue. *Ugh…* He ran the cold water and splashed his face and chest for a bit, hoping it would liven him up some. He could go back to bed. There was nothing pressing at the precinct. The captain had told him and Martin McCready, his partner, to take the day off, so why not take advantage of it? Maybe a cup of coffee first.

His cell buzzed as he made his way to the kitchen. He pretended not to see the trail of clothes he'd left strewn across the bedroom floor. After a glance at the ID screen he croaked, "Hey, Martin. What's up?"

His partner's chuckle was followed by, "You sound real chipper this morning."

"I might be after a caffeine fix. How're you doing?"

"Fine and dandy. Better than you by the sounds of it. Of course, I didn't stay till closing time like I'm guessing you did."

"And I wouldn't have if I had a beautiful wife and kids to go home to." Sam tucked his phone against his ear so he could prep the coffee machine and talk at the same time.

Another chuckle. "That would make headline news."

"Smartass. So why are you calling me so damned early?"

"It's almost *ten*, Sam. Liz wanted to know if you'd like to have dinner with us tonight. Think you can handle a home-cooked meal for a change?"

"Hey, I cook…"

"Yeah, anything that comes frozen or canned." Martin tsked. "I don't know how you keep in such good shape eating all that crap all the time. Anyway, Liz is making meatloaf, her mama's recipe, the one you had three helpings of last time. Abe and Sara still talk about Unca Sam putting it all away. Sara wanted to know why you don't have a belly like mine."

Sam smiled as he spooned the coffee into the filter. "Metabolism, I guess. Plus, three workouts a week, at which you could join me if you wished. And the answer is yes, I would love to have dinner with y'all. What time and what can I bring?"

"Forget the workouts. Raising a family is enough of a workout for me. Six, and you don't have to bring anything. You know that. And especially all that stuff you always bring to spoil the kids with."

"Okay, six it is," Sam said, ignoring Martin's last remark. "Looking forward to it, Martin. Thanks."

Waiting for the coffee to brew, he counted himself lucky to have a partner like Martin McCready. A lot of detectives had good partners, but Sam always felt he'd struck gold with Martin. An African-American, tall with big shoulders and big fists, a good guy to have with him in tight corners, but also sane, with no judgment and a great sense of humor. Sam was sure that no matter what, Martin had his back, and when it came down to it, he had Martin's, no questions asked. He'd heard the expression about taking a bullet for someone, and he thought he really would for his partner…without a doubt.

Plus, he had the added bonus of being included in the McCready family. He had none of his own, being one of those teens thrown out for being gay—and maybe he overcompensated by bringing Martin's kids 'stuff' every time he visited, but what the hey? He'd been banned from seeing his own niece and nephew so he couldn't spoil *them. Their loss,* he'd told himself a hundred times over the years, but deep down, sometimes it still hurt.

Sam's dad had stared at him, his face mottling to a dark red. *'You are*—what *did you say?'*

'I'm gay, Dad. I want you and Mom to be okay with it. I know it's probably a shock, but I don't want to live a lie. I want—'

The punch to his jaw had taken him by surprise. He hadn't gone down, but he'd staggered backward, staring at his father in complete shock.

'You fuckin' faggot,' his father had screamed. *'You are everything that is vile and loathsome. You are condemned by God and you will get the fuck outta my house right now.'*

'Dad!'

'I am not your dad. Not anymore, and you are not my son, now get out. Thank God your mother and your sister's not home to listen to this.'

Tears had sprung to Sam's eyes. His jaw had throbbed, but it had been the hatred in his father's expression that had caused him to sob. *'Dad, you don't mean this, you can't—'*

'I mean every fucking word, now get out—get out!'

He had wanted to tell him that his friend Kenny had come out to his parents a few days ago and they'd been okay with it, telling him they loved him no matter what. That was what had encouraged him to tell his folks. Never had he anticipated this kind of reaction. Just two days ago, his dad had come to the ballpark and had cheered him on with everyone else when he'd thrown the Hail Mary that had won them the game. But now, the outrage that had darkened his father's face had told him he didn't want to listen to any kind of explanation.

He had run up to his room and stuffed his backpack with some clothes and his textbooks. Jim Walker had been waiting for him at the foot of the stairs.

'You take nothing with you.'

'I have to have clothes, Dad, and I need my books for school.'

'I said nothing!'

He'd grabbed for Sam's backpack, but Sam wouldn't let go. They'd tussled, his father had tripped and fallen on his ass and Sam had made for the door. His father had become a raving lunatic and Sam had needed his stuff. He'd grabbed his bike that was lying on the driveway, vaulted onto it and taken off down the street, his dad's hate-filled words following him until he'd turned the corner and could no longer hear him.

Sam shook his head to clear his mind of those ghastly memories. Shit, why would a call from Martin send his mind spinning into that vortex of hate? Bad enough that the case they'd closed only yesterday had been brutal.

Long hours tracking the suspects, days of frustration when it looked like they couldn't get enough to justify an arrest, then, like in a lot of cases, the unsubs had gotten careless. One of the victims had managed to escape and there they'd been, Sam and Martin, ready to scoop the little girl up and listen to her directions to where the creeps had been holding her and her sister. Busting up that child-slave ring had been one of the more rewarding moments of Sam and Martin's lives, along with the other cops they'd used as backup. Sam had relished putting his fist on the jaw of the fat slob terrorizing the kid's sister and the other little ones being held in that vile place.

When the rest of the felons had been rounded up, cuffed, charged and locked away pending a court date, Sam had felt in need of a drink and had voiced that opinion long and loud.

'*Just one,*' he'd lied. It had taken more than one to help him forget, for the time being at least, the state of those little kids, the fear etched on their faces and the sheer trembling relief when they realized they'd been saved from whatever hell their kidnappers had in store for them. So, he'd overdone it a bit and was now paying the price. The coffee tasted good though…damned good.

He sank down on the couch and tuned the TV into the morning local news. Yep, there it was, the coverage on the kiddy slave ring. The police chief up there giving the reporters what they wanted to hear, kids reunited with their families after weeks of anguish, pics of the little tykes—*How in hell could any human being even think of selling these pretty girls, or any kid, to some slavering sex monster?* God, but he'd wanted to rip the heads off the slavers. It was of some consolation that those pigs would have a really rough time in prison. Guys in there had their own code of justice, especially when it came to dealing with those responsible for child molestation. *Oh, and a picture of me without Martin…he'll be pissed. Heh, heh…*

His cell buzzed and he reached for it. Not a number or name he recognized. *Robertson, Justin*?

"Sam Walker."

"Hi, Sam." The voice was nice, but he didn't recognize it…or did he?

"Hi…uh, Justin? Do I know you?"

"Um, well…uh, you did last night."

"Last night?" Sam searched his memory banks. *I met this guy last night?*

Justin laughed lightly. "Well you were kinda drunk, but I'm hurt you don't remember me. You kissed me. Guess you don't remember that either."

I kissed him? He thought harder. After Martin had left—and he did remember that, some of the other guys had split too and he—that was right, he'd taken a cab over to the Blue Bar on Santa Monica.

"Uh…were you at the Blue Bar?"

"Ah, it's starting to come back." Justin laughed again…a nice laugh, low and throaty. "I was sitting at the bar, you came in, smiled at me, sat next to me, bought me a drink. We talked. You said you were a cop. Or was that a come-on? Are you a cop?"

"Uh, no, not a come-on. Uh, yeah I'm a cop…detective."

"Okay, so we talked for some time. I figured at some point it was getting late and when I looked at my watch you said, 'don't go', and you kissed me."

Shit. Why couldn't he remember? And what the hell else did he do—or rather, try to do? "Uh, wow, I'm sorry."

"Sorry you don't remember me or sorry you kissed me?"

"Both, I guess. Hope I didn't come on too obnoxious."

That laugh again…so sexy. *Why can't I put a face to it?* "No, you didn't. I said I had to go and you wanted my phone number, so we traded. After you kissed me you said, 'call me'. So here I am, calling you."

"And I bet you didn't expect this kind of response. I'm sorry, Justin."

"Don't be, it's okay." His voice was gentle along with that trace of laughter. "You were kinda drunk, so…"

Sam groaned. "I'd like to make it up to you. Maybe meet for a drink sometime? I won't put any moves on you, promise."

"Well, where's the fun in that?" Justin's tone was a definite tease. "Now that you've offered, I would like to see you again…tonight? If that doesn't sound too pushy."

"Uh, can't tonight. I'm having dinner with my partner and his family."

"Oh, you have a partner?" Justin's chirpy voice sounded suddenly deflated. "Then I guess this isn't a good idea."

"No, no…not a *partner* partner. Working partner."

"Oh, okay. So what's good for you?"

"Well, I'd like to say tomorrow night, but I'd have to call you once I know what my schedule looks like."

"Sounds good."

"Uh, this is going to sound crass, I know, but can you describe yourself so I know who to look for when we fix a time and place?"

Justin's laughter was contagious. "Look in your phone, Detective. You took a selfie of us last night."

I did? "I did?" *Shit. This is beyond embarrassing. Just how hammered was I?* He stared at the photograph of himself and Justin. *How could I have forgotten what this hottie looks like?* Curly auburn hair and a smile that would light up the darkest room…or heart.

"Wow."

"Was that a good wow or a what-was-I-thinking wow?"

"That was a very good wow. And I look like a moron. What in hell were you thinking talking to me, anyway?"

"I thought you were cute."

Sam laughed. "Your powers of observation are a mite faulty. Sad thing is I look even worse today."

"How's that possible?"

"Hey!" He laughed again. "You're right. I promise to clean up my act for when we meet."

"I liked what I saw the first time around and I'm looking forward to seeing you again. Oops, gotta go, Sam. Duty calls. Bye."

"Oh, okay, bye." *Duty calls? What's that about?*

* * * *

Justin slid his cell into his pocket and jumped up from his desk when his boss barged into his office. "Where the hell are those designs, Justin?" Maria Esteban stared daggers at him. "You were supposed to have them on my desk first thing this morning. Where are they?"

"On your desk. They've been there since nine o'clock." He tried to keep the irritation out of his voice, replying as calmly as he could. *Why does she always have to be such a cow?*

"What?" She threw an accusatory glance over her shoulder at Paula Downs, her secretary, who had ambled in behind her. "Why didn't you tell me?"

Paula shrugged. "I thought you'd have noticed. Like Justin said, they've been there since nine. You were on the phone to Watson Industries. I thought you would've seen them then."

"Huh. Well, I didn't." She glared at Justin. "You should've flagged them for my attention or something."

Oh, so of course, it has to be my fault. "Maria—"

"Never mind." She cut him off. "I'll go look at them now, and I'll be back with them if they're not up to Esteban standard."

Justin closed his eyes and mentally counted to ten. When he opened them, Maria was gone and Paula was regarding him with sympathy.

"Don't take it personally. She's in a foul mood this morning."

"No kidding." He sighed. "This morning and every morning. Don't know how much longer I can take this."

"Don't you even think of quitting." Paula walked over to his desk. "Justin, you are the best we have...have ever had, if that makes sense. And she knows it too."

"Yeah, but being the best designer of ladies' and kiddies' *apparel* is not something I want to be doing for the rest of my life."

"I know, you want into one of the big fashion houses, and you deserve it. Just consider this a good training ground, and"—Paula grinned at him—"learning to deal with the likes of her is also good training for when you have to go rounds with real bitches."

Justin chuckled. "You're probably right. But what are the bets she won't say a word about the new designs, good or bad?"

"Well, we know they're not *bad*. She'll like 'em."

After Paula left, Justin glanced at his watch. After eleven. He could head out for lunch and deal with Maria when he got back. *No point in getting upset with her.* Paula was right. If he could deal with the fiery Puerto Rican lady, he could deal with just about anyone. It wasn't a bad job. He'd had worse and had considered himself lucky when he'd been hired by Esteban Fashions. It was a step in the right direction toward the bigger fashion houses, if he could make the grade.

The coffee house on the first floor of the building that housed Esteban Fashions and a dozen or so other businesses wasn't busy and, after ordering a tuna sandwich and a hot tea, he sat at a table near the window and cast his mind back to the night before.

He was miffed the hot cop didn't remember him. Well, he'd been more than just a little tipsy. Still, he'd thought there might have been some semblance of a memory of the kiss he'd laid on Justin's lips. A kiss that had stolen Justin's breath and a piece of his mind. A great kiss and one he wasn't going to forget anytime soon. Too bad it hadn't had the same effect on Detective Walker.

He wondered if he'd ever hear from him again. *This time the cop's going to have to call me…* He'd made the first move—now it was up to the detective to show some interest, if he had any. Maybe during the day he'd get little flashes of the time they'd spent together at the Blue Bar. It had been crazy hot, sitting there leaning into each other, Sam's face mere inches from his own, his full lips so tantalizingly near, his smile a little off kilter from the booze, but sexy nevertheless, and that body… Muscles clearly defined under his shirt, the sleeves turned up revealing strong, slightly hairy forearms.

He was getting hard just thinking about the guy. Harder when he thought about the kiss they'd shared. Those soft, warm lips, the glide of his tongue when they'd opened to each other, the way Sam had pushed into the kiss as if he'd never wanted it to end.

And neither did I. He could have gone on and on into the wee small hours just taking my mouth, making it his own. Dammit, but I want a repeat performance…and soon!

Chapter Two

On his way over to Martin's house, Sam stopped by the Glendale Mall and picked up a *Star Wars* coloring book for Abe and a crafts embroidery kit for Sara, her latest hobby. He made sure the kit was for a six-year old and he threw in a couple of *Star Wars* action figures at the last minute. Abe already had quite a collection, but Sam was sure he didn't have these two from the latest movie. Browsing the kid's store took his mind off Justin at least for the few minutes it took to grab the stuff and head for the register.

Driving toward Martin and Liz's home, he reflected that the guy had hardly been out of his mind all day ever since the phone call to end all phone calls. *Surprised much?* And how humiliating for the guy to be told *nope, I don't remember you at all*. He should have called him later and told him *yes, now that I'm starting to think about last night, I am remembering some things about you. About how that curly hair flopped over your brow from time to time and I'd actually had the nerve – booze-induced of course – to brush it back with my fingertips*.

And I do remember that kiss. I thought it was the drinks that had made me dizzy, but it was the taste of your mouth and the warmth of your lips – and shit, now I'm getting hard for like the third time today – and that never happens – just from remembering bits and pieces of our time together. I wonder what we'd have done if I hadn't been so hammered. Would you have come back to my place, or I to yours? Would we have made love all night or would I have been unable to do anything about it like I usually am, and you'd have sighed and said so long, Sam?

God, but I'm a mess.

He pulled up outside the McCready residence, honked the horn then grinned when Abe and Sara came running out to meet him. He loved these kids and he loved the fact that they were always so quick to hug him when he got down on his knees and held his arms open for them. He might be a rough and tough cop when needed, but he loved affection just like anybody else. And the dearth of that in his life made him a sucker for little Sara's kisses on his cheek while Abe jumped on his back and yelled "Giddy-up!"

"Will you let Sam get in the house before you start all those shenanigans?" Martin yelled from the doorway. Sam got to his feet, carrying Sara with him and holding one of Abe's hands so he didn't slide off.

"Don't know about these kids of yours, McCready. They are way too grabby." He turned around so Martin could lift Abe off his back. Sara giggled and held on tight to his neck as he followed Martin inside. "Oh, I forgot the goody-bag. It's in the car." He wheeled around, spinning Sara with him. She shrieked and hung on tightly, giggling all the way to the car.

"Sam must be here," Liz said when he re-entered, carrying a still-giggling Sara.

"Hi, beautiful." Sam put Sara down and leaned in to kiss Liz's cheek. Her honey-dark skin was silky smooth and, when she hugged him, her body felt soft and curvaceous. Elizabeth McCready was a beautiful woman, so gorgeous that Sam had teased Martin many times with the line, 'How did you ever manage to persuade Liz to marry you?'

"Mmm, you smell so good," he murmured.

"Hey, stop sniffing my wife."

Sam chortled. "You want I should sniff you instead?"

"At your peril."

"Unca Sam…" Abe was clinging to Sam's leg. "Unca Sam."

"I didn't forget you, buddy. Here." He handed the four-year-old the coloring book and action figures, grinning when the kid whooped and rushed away to his room.

"Say thank you," Liz called after him.

"Thank you, Unca Sam," Abe shouted.

Martin shook his head as Sam handed the craft kit to Sara. "I told you last time you're spoiling them."

"Oh, so you don't want the wine?"

"Gimme that."

Liz rolled her eyes when Martin grabbed the bottle and headed for the kitchen. "You look nice," she said. "New shirt?"

Sam fingered the blue cotton polo, a recent purchase. He nodded. "Macy's on sale."

"Martin tells me you had quite the night out with the boys." She took Sam's hand and led him over to the couch.

Sam grimaced. At least his partner didn't know about his routine at the Blue Bar, kissing a guy and taking selfies then not remembering who the heck he was.

"Yeah, I kinda overdid it, I guess. I think it was just the relief of finally bringing those creeps down and knowing that those kids were going home."

"I can't imagine how anyone could do that to those little girls." Liz shuddered and gazed at Sara sitting by their feet and laying out the pieces of the sewing kit.

Sam patted her hand. "I know, but at least this time we were able to get them a happy ending. Trouble is there's more in every major city. We just have to be vigilant."

"But those kids were taken from church, Sam. Who would ever dream of that happening?"

"Hey, Sam…" Martin called out from the kitchen. "You want some o' this or a beer?"

"Just a half glass of wine, thanks. Gotta take it easy after last night."

"Hair of the dog," his partner quipped, handing him a glass. "How 'bout you, honey?"

"This is good," Sam said, grinning.

"Smartass."

"Martin!" Liz glared at her husband then flicked her gaze to Sara.

"Sorry. Would you like a glass of wine, dear wife?"

"I'll wait till we eat, but you go right ahead. I still have stuff to do in the kitchen."

"Can I help?" Sam asked.

"No. You guys sit and shoot the breeze, and…" She gave Martin the fish-eye. "Watch your language."

Sam chuckled—his partner looked suitably cowed. He leaned back into the comfortable couch cushions and gazed around the living room. "You've changed some stuff," he said.

Martin nodded. "Liz got into a redecorating mode a couple of weeks back. Changed the color of the dining room walls and hung some new drapes."

"All by herself?"

Martin nodded again. "She is Superwoman. I said I'd pay for a painter, but she wanted to DIY. Says it relaxes her." He took a sip of his wine then asked, "You catch the news earlier?"

"Yeah. Not often I get the feeling of a job well done, but it did feel good knowing those creeps will be behind bars for a long, long time."

"Not long enough," Martin growled.

"I hear ya."

"And how come they had a picture of you and not me?"

"Dunno. Maybe they just figured I'm the prettier of the two of us."

Martin let out a snorting laugh. "I'll let you get away with that, but only 'cause it's true."

"Anyway, it's good that we busted that bunch of lowlifes," Sam said with relish then took a long sip of his wine.

"It makes me wonder just what the fu—I mean what'll be next for us to deal with." He looked guiltily at Sara, but she was too engrossed in her craft to notice his near-slip.

"Okay, boys, to the table please," Liz sang out. "Martin, go get Abe and make sure his hands are clean."

"Yes, boss."

The meal Liz had prepared was delicious and Sam kept his reputation intact by being able to have more helpings than anyone else. Abe stared at him in awe, watching him devour his third helping. As far as Sam was concerned, it was the perfect antidote for a queasy stomach.

"Sorry," he mumbled after cleaning his plate. "Guess I took care of your leftovers."

Liz chuckled. "My mama, if she was alive, would've been tickled pink to see you enjoy her meatloaf."

Abe stretched his mouth with a gigantic yawn and Liz told Martin, "Why don't you get the kids ready for bed while Sam helps me clear up in here?"

Martin pushed his chair back and stood. "C'mon, kids, give your Unca Sam goodnight kisses then off to bed."

Neither of them protested and Sara almost fell asleep in Sam's arms when he held her for their goodnight kiss. "They are the best," he told Liz as they cleared the table.

"They're pretty good most of the time." Liz gathered up the dinner plates and took them into the kitchen. Sam followed, carrying some of the glasses. "Just put 'em on the counter, Sam, while I stack the dishwasher." He went out and collected the rest then watched Liz rinse some of the plates before placing them in the washer.

"So..." She dried her hands on a towel and gave Sam a meaningful look. He knew what was coming. "How've you been?"

"Oh, I'm sure Martin keeps you up-to-date with what we're doing."

"I don't mean that."

Of course you don't.

"I mean your private, personal life. Not so private of course if you're gonna tell me what you're up to."

"Do I have to?"

Liz chuckled. "No, but I was hoping you'd tell me you'd met someone so you could forget all about that skunk you used to hang out with."

"Liz, I'm over him. That was two years ago."

"And there hasn't been anyone since?"

"No one that's got me fired up enough to ask them for a date."

Liz tutted. "That's just not natural. Don't you have *needs*?"

Sam laughed. "If you think I'm going to tell you about my *needs*, you must be crazy."

"Oh, so you do have them, then?"

"Well, yes, when I let myself think about it, I guess." His face felt suddenly warm as the vision of a guy with curly auburn hair and a terrific smile swam before his eyes.

"Are you all right, Sam?" Liz sounded concerned. "You've gone really red in the face."

"What? No…yeah, I'm fine."

"I'm sorry, did my mentioning Daryl upset you?"

"No, not at all, but…" He glanced at his watch. "I should get going. Thanks for that great meal, Liz. Sorry I made a pig of myself…again."

"You're welcome. Are you sure you're all right?"

"Yes." He hugged her and kissed her cheek. "And thanks for caring."

"Always. Go tell your partner g'bye."

Daryl. He hadn't thought about that cheating jerk in a while, and Liz saying his name hadn't been a pleasant experience. Too many memories of bitter words, of recriminations on both sides. Some resentment still clung at times, and there were moments when he imagined confronting the son-of-a-bitch and throwing a few choice words in his face. But what would be the point of that? All the things he should have said at the time would now just sound petty and, yes, mean-spirited. No matter how true, it would still come across like a jealous rant.

"You're better than that," he told himself as he pulled his BMW into the apartment building's parking lot. Daryl, he'd heard through the grapevine, had married the guy he'd left Sam for and was now living in Seattle. So, in essence he was completely out of Sam's life.

And a good thing too.

Once inside his spartan apartment, he flung off his clothes, heaping them onto a chair in the bedroom, and slipped on a clean pair of boxer shorts. *A beer sounds good right now, but just the one.* As he popped the can and took a long chug of the cold brew, he wondered what Justin was doing right then. Would it be awkward if he called just to say hi? He slumped down on his couch, picked up his cell and thumbed through until he found the selfie he'd taken of himself and Justin. What had he been thinking at that moment? This was so out of character for him, cozying up to a complete stranger, taking a picture of him and *kissing* him, for cripessake.

What the hell. The guy couldn't think too badly of him. *He called me after all.* He hit Justin's number then almost hung up when the ring tone started. *Get a fucking grip.*

"Hey, this is a surprise." Justin sounded genuinely pleased.

"Uh, yeah. I was just thinking about you and wondering if I had apologized enough for my crass behavior, and for not remembering who you were."

Justin's throaty chuckle stirred something inside Sam and before he realized what he was doing he was stroking himself while listening to Justin telling him he was fine with the way they'd left things and hoping they could get together…real soon.

"Uh, yeah, soon as I know what they've got lined up for me at the precinct. Uh, how was your day?"

"Kind of shitty actually, so it's good to hear your voice instead of the harsh tones of my boss complaining about stuff."

"What do you do?"

"Design apparel for an independent fashion house."

"Wow, that sounds interesting."

Justin's laughter was low and sexy and Sam's cock, hardening in his hand, pulsed at the sound of it. "No, it doesn't, not to a detective anyway. I'm sure yours is a lot more interesting. I saw that great picture of you on the TV, by the way…you being commended for busting up that child-trafficking ring. Good for you."

"Yeah, it felt good. You have a nice voice, Justin."

"So do you. Nice and deep and butch, and I love that twang I hear now and then. Where are you from?"

Sam chuckled. He was enjoying this. It had been a long time since he'd held a flirtatious phone call with a guy. "Uh, Texas originally."

"I thought so. Big things come from Texas, I hear." They laughed together then Justin said, "I'm really looking forward to seeing you again, Detective." His sexy voice purred in Sam's ear.

"Me, too, and it's Sam."

"Sam. I like it."

"How do you like it?" Oh now, he was getting carried away, but his cock was so darned hard and soaking his boxers.

"Any way you want to give it to me, Sam, long as it comes with a lot of your sexy kisses."

"Really?"

"Oh God, yeah. When I close my eyes and remember your arms around me, your lips so soft and warm on mine, your tongue doing amazing things, there's nothing quite like it."

"It was that good?" Did his voice sound as strained to Justin as it did to him?

"Better than good, Sam. The best."

Oh, my God. His hand was working overtime and his cock had never been this hard…ever. And getting harder by the second just from listening to the sultry tones of a guy who, until this morning, he had no memory of ever meeting. Any more of this and he was going to come, crazy though it was.

"Uh, Justin, I have to co—I mean go. I'll call you tomorrow. Is that okay?"

"Absolutely. G'night…Sam."

"G'night." He pulled his cock free of his boxer shorts just in time. A stream of cum shot across his heaving chest and he groaned out loud, his body shuddering from its release. *Shit.* What the hell was that about? This never happened to him, not without some chemical stimulation, and even then it could be iffy. He'd given up jacking off as a lost cause a long time ago…and now?

All this from just the sound of the guy's voice. If Justin came through with the chance of another meeting, holding and kissing him *again* was going to feel like Nirvana.

Chapter Three

"You look cheery this morning."

Justin looked up when Maria's secretary, Paula, entered his office. "Almost glad to be here."

He smiled. "I decided there's no point in hating every minute of my time at work. Besides, I might have a date tonight. First one in months."

"Oh yes? Who's the lucky guy?"

"Someone I met a couple of nights ago. He was in his cups, to put it mildly, but so darned hot I couldn't tell him to get lost when he came on to me."

Paula frowned. "You sure you want to go out with another drunk, Justin?"

Justin had shared with Paula his disastrous relationship with Brad, an alcoholic Justin had thought he could perhaps persuade to get counseling or join Alcoholics Anonymous. Brad hadn't given sobriety much of a shot, falling off the wagon more times than Justin could count and, after a horrendous fight during which Brad had struck Justin hard across the face, Justin had decided enough was enough and had moved out.

There hadn't been anyone in his life since, and he hadn't missed the irony of finding yet another drunk attractive. Although this time he was pretty sure Sam wasn't a habitual drunkard.

"Don't worry," he told Paula. "We've talked since then, and sober he sounds even more terrific."

"Hmm, okay. Oh, not to cast gloom on your day, but the boss lady wants to see you in her office at ten o'clock."

"She gonna give me a raise?"

"Ha! Nope, that didn't come up in the conversation. But you can always ask for one."

Paula left and Justin opened his laptop to the latest designs he'd done for Esteban. They were some of his best work and Maria had been less than complimentary. He had a sneaking suspicion that she didn't praise him because she didn't want to increase his salary or let him think he was too good for Esteban Fashions. One thing he knew for certain was that if he decided to leave, she'd never give him a glowing reference.

He frowned. *Okay, stop getting pissed off.* There was a chance he'd have a date with a hunky detective this evening and he didn't want to show up trailing the vestiges of a bad mood behind him. Sam had surprised him last night, and by using the flimsiest of excuses about not being sure if he'd apologized enough for not remembering meeting him or kissing him. His so-deep voice had sent goosebumps all over Justin's skin and just listening to him had made him hard. He had an idea Sam had been hard, too. His voice had gotten a little strained toward the end of their conversation, as if he was trying to hold something back—like an orgasm maybe.

He chuckled. Well, Sam wouldn't have been the only one. Justin had had to jerk off, too, after they'd done talking. Of course, he maybe had more to work with than Sam. He could remember every little detail about the hunky cop. Those brilliant blue eyes and that lush mouth and the cleft in his chin deep enough to stick the tip of his tongue into if he'd had the nerve.

Maybe he should've confessed up front that he was turned on and engaged the hot detective in some mutual phone sex. *How great would that have been!*

* * * *

Sam moved over to Martin's desk when Captain Hoskins announced he had a couple of new cases for them all to listen to. "I want y'all to know what's going on. I'll allocate duties after I've filled y'all in. Last night the 7-Eleven on Robson was held up. Three guys, or maybe two guys and a female—the clerk wasn't sure—wearing masks and armed with shotguns killed the store manager and a female customer. They got away with the contents of the registers and the safe. They shot the place up real good—the clerk is lucky he's alive. We have the surveillance tapes and from what I've seen, one of the perps could be a young woman…slighter build, not that it means anything really, just an impression."

"Is it suspicious that the clerk was left unarmed?" Sam asked.

"He's being questioned as we speak," Hoskins said. "Jones and Harrison, I want you to take this one, okay?"

There was a chorus of mumbled 'okays'.

"Okay, next. Walker and McCready, listen up. I want you guys on this one. A young man was found murdered in a deli's delivery doorway off Santa Monica. The owner called it in. No ID on him, no money either, so the motive could've been robbery. Could be a hustler. There's a park near where the body was found frequented by hustlers, male prostitutes and the like.

"Regardless of our personal feelings about cases like this, if there's murder or kidnapping involved we have to put a stop to it. Detectives, I suggest you get over to that park at night, talk to these kids, get them to trust you enough to give you some leads. Come to my office after this briefing and I'll give you more details."

Sam heard a voice from somewhere in the back of the room say, "Should be a piece of cake for Walker. A fag'll fit right in."

Martin must have heard it too. He stiffened and turned to face the guys behind them. "Who said that?"

Sam tugged his sleeve. "Don't go there, Martin. It's just ignorance talking."

"And cowardice too, seein' as how no one's admitting to it. I hear crap like that again and *whoever* will be talkin' to my fist."

"Detectives," Hoskins barked. "My office, now."

"You gonna let whoever it was get away with that?" Martin demanded once they were inside Hoskins' office. "What happened to zero tolerance?"

"No, I'm not, but I'll deal with it according to regulations," Hoskins said. "You start a fist fight in the department and I'll deal with you, too."

"Calm down, Martin." Sam grinned at him. "When we find out who it is, we'll just take him out back and beat the shit outta him."

Hoskins frowned. "Just as well I know you're joking. Okay, here's a shot of the kid, post-mortem." He pushed a picture across his desk.

Sam gazed at the dead boy and his gut twisted. "He was strangled."

Hoskins nodded. "Looks like it."

"Kind of strange for a robbery, don't you think?" Martin remarked. "Usually it's pretty much bash and grab."

Sam grunted agreement. "Or it was some john who didn't wanna pay up. Started to rough the kid up and it got out of hand."

"So that's for you guys to find out," Hoskins said. "This is gonna be mostly a night shift for you. I'll pencil you in four to midnight for the next few days. Now go talk to the coroner."

* * * *

Ron Barrett, the coroner on duty, was his usual cool and efficient self when he opened the storage drawer containing the dead hustler's body. Sam knew Ron had seen countless bodies in the years he'd been a coroner—young, old, male, female—but it still irked him that the man could be so apparently unmoved by what he saw on a daily basis. Sam had been a cop for eight years, but he still couldn't regard a dead body as just a piece of meat to be cut open to establish the cause of death. At least, in this instance, there would be no need to mutilate this body. The cause of death was immediately visible. The bruises around his neck gave witness to a brutal strangling.

"He put up a good fight," Ron said indicating further bruising on the dead boy's arms and chest. "From the state of his knuckles, I'd say he got some hard punches in before he succumbed. You'll be looking for someone with prodigious strength. The larynx is completely crushed…"

"Any fragments under his nails?" Sam asked

Ron nodded. "Yeah. No skin but a bit of a mixture of fibers, like there had been more than one person involved."

"Could be from one or more of his johns," Martin said flatly.

"Were there traces of semen in his mouth?" Sam asked.

"No, but of course they might have been washed away if he had something to drink. There could be vestiges in his stomach if as you said he'd been with a couple of men, but no autopsy has been ordered so far."

And it's unlikely to be as the cause of death is so evident.

"This might be of interest." Ron produced a small plastic bag. "I separated what we found under his fingernails. This thread is tougher than you'd find on a regular jacket or coat. I'm guessing a uniform of some kind."

Sam and Martin exchanged glances. "Like a military uniform?"

"Yes, or just about anything made of a thicker material."

Sam stared at the contusions on the boy's face. No doubt that despite the marring bruises he had once been a good-looking kid. *God, but sometimes I hate this job.* "Wait." He leaned in for a closer look. "He's only wearing one earring."

"Could be a fashion statement," Martin suggested.

"But the other ear is also pierced."

"Could have been pulled out in the struggle," Ron said. He peered at the left ear. "Slight inflammation around the piercing. You're right—he probably was wearing one in each ear."

"Doesn't really help much, unfortunately."

"Poor kid." Martin sighed. "What in hell did he do to get himself killed?"

Sam nudged Martin's arm. "We need to get over to that park and see if any of those guys will talk to us."

Sam realized that whatever he and Justin were planning, it wasn't going to happen tonight, but he thought he should call him and let him know the reason.

Justin sounded disappointed, and Sam knew he should not be happy about that.

"Oh, well, you did say you wouldn't know your schedule until today," he said, the tone in his voice a shade wistful. "We'll take a raincheck, right?"

"Right. Martin and I are on a new case, so it could be a while."

"Oh, wow." Justin's sigh made Sam feel bad.

Maybe if we finish early enough… "How's your day been so far?" he asked.

"Awful. I had a bit of a run-in with the boss. She was rude. More than rude really, pretty crass. I told her to go fuck herself."

Sam laughed. "You still have a job?"

"Just about, and only because she knows she can't find anyone as good as me for the money she's paying. Sorry, did that sound arrogant?"

"Not at all. A guy should know his worth. What was she rude about?"

"I'll have to tell you another time." Justin had lowered his voice. "I can hear her outside my office, and she doesn't sound too happy. I better go."

"Okay, bye."

Sam ended the call feeling that somehow, he'd just become involved in a part of Justin's life he knew as little of as he did of the man himself. He couldn't help but think their first meeting—that is, one he would actually remember—would be at the very least memorable.

* * * *

Their first stop was the deli where the body had been found. The owner, Lennie Cohen, still seemed a little shaken up while they talked to him.

"I couldn't believe it, the poor kid," Cohen told them, his pale blue eyes watery. "What a way to start my morning. Bad enough I had deliveries to cope with and him lying there…it was…I don't know how to say it. What will his poor mama do when you tell her?"

Sam had a feeling there would be no 'poor mama' to tell of her son's death. Another lost boy, like so many on the streets of Los Angeles.

That night, they staked out the park behind Santa Monica Boulevard and the narrow streets that surrounded it. For a time, they watched the few young men cruising the area. One, a tall, slender blond kid, took a long look into their car, his expression showing interest as he gazed at Sam. Then, as if a sixth sense had kicked in, he stiffened, looked away and quickened his pace as he passed the car.

Martin chuckled. "Guess even your handsome mug can't disguise the fact you're a cop."

"Very funny." Sam sat back and grimaced. "It kinda tears me up to think what they go through just to stay alive."

"They could get a job," Martin said. "A real job. One that doesn't put them at risk from predators or get them arrested."

"It isn't always that easy. I know."

"But you didn't turn to hustling."

"No, but I have to admit I was tempted a couple of times. Nothing like an empty belly and a hard sidewalk to make you rethink a lot of things. If it hadn't been for the few friends I had left, I might have ended up like that kid."

His cell buzzed and he grunted as he stared at the screen. "Huh, coroner's office. Detective Walker."

"Oh hi, Detective. Dale Hawkins, assistant coroner. We have an ID on the murder victim you're investigating. His name is Joey Carter, age eighteen, no known street address in L.A. Originally from Dayton, Ohio."

"Any parents, siblings?"

"None on record, I'm afraid. The address in Dayton didn't pan out. Looks like it'll be a rough case for you."

"Right. Okay, thanks for the info." He ended the call and turned to face Martin. "Vic's name is Joey Carter, eighteen years old, homeless by the sounds of it and no next of kin on record."

Martin grimaced. "Shit, poor kid."

"Well, now that we have a name, we can ask around and see if any of these guys knew him."

"If we can get them to talk to us."

Sam slipped out of the car when another young man approached. He pulled out his badge. "Detective Sam Walker, LAPD. You have a minute?"

The guy reared back in surprise. "What's this about? I haven't done anything."

"That's okay, I just have a few questions. What's your name?"

"Rolando Lopez." He was slim and dark-haired, wearing a skintight T-shirt and skinny jeans. A good-looking kid with fine features and light gray eyes.

"Rolando, did you know Joey Carter?"

He nodded. "Yeah. All of us around here knew Joey. He was a sweet kid, kinda crazy sometimes, but…" He broke off and swiped at his eyes. "Sorry, can't believe he's gone. You know who killed him?"

"Not yet. We're looking for leads, anything you can tell us."

"I'm surprised you cops are bothering to investigate. Guys get roughed up around here and no one gives a shit."

"This is murder, Rolando. We intend to find out who did it and put them away. Now, can you tell me who Joey was close to, apart from yourself?"

"We weren't that close really, but a kid called Mikey was pretty tight with Joey. I haven't seen him around tonight."

"Mikey… He have a last name?"

"Probably, but I don't know it."

"Can you describe him for me?"

"He's kinda short, fair hair, got a pug nose, but he's cute, I guess. Look, I have to get moving. Good luck finding the son of a bitch that killed Joey." He took off before Sam could ask him anything else. Then again, he reckoned he'd gotten as much from the kid as he was likely to get.

"He know anything?" Martin asked as Sam settled in the passenger seat.

"Not really. There's a kid called Mikey that Joey was tight with, according to Rolando, the guy I was talking to. Mikey's short with fair hair and a pug nose."

Martin chuckled. "That's some description. Maybe we should try the other side of the park, see if there's more action over there. Seems like a slow night to me."

"Joey's murder might have made some of the kids more cautious," Sam said. Martin put the car in gear and cruised to the far side of the park. "We could check out one of their hang-out joints. That coffee shop on the corner looks likely."

"Okay."

When Sam and Martin entered Pete's Coffee Place, a lot of wary gazes zeroed in on them. Sam could tell they'd been identified as cops regardless of the jeans and T-shirts they were wearing. Martin had told him he figured it was that in most people's opinion guys as big as them were either cops or bad guys. Sam grinned when four men got up out of their booth and exited the coffee shop.

"We're bad for business," he told Martin.

A young Latino wearing some kind of uniform approached them. "Can I help you guys?"

Sam pulled out his badge. "Detective Walker and this is Detective McCready. We want to talk to anyone who knew Joey Carter." He said it loud enough for everyone in the small café to hear. "Anyone here knew Joey?"

A blond kid sitting with two others in a booth put his hand up. "We knew Joey."

Sam and Martin approached the table and the kids eyed them both, blatantly checking them out. "Can you answer a few questions for us?" Sam asked.

"Sure," the blond said, dragging his gaze from Sam's face to his crotch and back again.

Martin growled. "You wanna join us at that bigger table over there." He pointed to the corner of the café.

The three crawled out of the booth and followed them over to the table. "So, wanna give us your names?" Sam flipped open his notebook.

"I'm Armie Hammer." The blond winked at Sam.

"I'm Henry Cavill." The second kid smiled at Martin.

"And I'm Matt Damon." The third one pushed his ass back into his seat and thrust his crotch upward.

Martin slammed his meaty hand down on the table, hard, and made them all jump. 'Matt' almost fell off his seat. "And I've had enough of the bullshit," Martin hissed, looking like a fierce Samuel L. Jackson. "You think this is a game? Your buddy, Joey, was murdered, strangled to death so hard his larynx was crushed. You think that's funny, huh?"

"No." The blond flicked a nervous glance at Sam.

"Okay, let's have your real names this time." Sam poised his pen over an open page.

"Uh, I'm Albie…Albie Schenk. This is Phil and Randy."

"Last names." He wrote them down as they recited Johnson and McGarry. "Okay, so how well did you know Joey?"

Albie shrugged. "He hung out with us some nights if we weren't y'know, uh, busy. He was a bit of a loner though."

"Him and Mikey were better buds," the one called Phil said. "And Clyde. They roomed together when they had the money."

"Have you seen Mikey tonight?" Martin asked.

They all shook their heads. "He goes to other parks, well, we all do really," Albie said. "Sometimes it gets rough around here and we have to move on, stay out of the way of the gangs that want to beat the shit out of us."

Sam sighed. "Did Joey have any enemies?"

"Don't think so, apart from like the ones we all have," Phil told him. "Those fuckin' thugs that come around now and then. Punk kids just lookin' to bash a fag. Bastards."

They left the boys in the café without much to work on. Sam hadn't really been expecting to get a lead to the killer from them. If anything, they seemed to take his death as unsurprising in a way. A danger that all of them faced by having sex with complete strangers, getting into cars without knowing the driver's identity, perhaps being beaten by some self-loathing closet case. Sam's gut twisted at the thought of it all.

There but for the grace of the God I don't believe in, go I…

"So, call it a night?" Martin shifted restlessly in his seat.

"Yeah, guess so. We can come back tomorrow night and look for this Mikey kid everyone seems to think was Joey's closest friend. I'll drop you off home."

"Thank you, my man, very generous of you."

They chuckled together as Sam pulled the car away from the curb.

Chapter Four

After he'd delivered Martin to his front door, Sam wondered if Justin would still be up…maybe for just another conversation, and this time, he told himself, *Control your libido! Never thought I'd have to tell myself that…*

He punched in Justin's saved number.

"Hey, Sam." Justin sounded pleased to hear from him and that made Sam feel kinda warm inside.

"Did your day get any better?"

"Not really, but I don't want to talk about that. Sounds like so much whining really."

"You can whine on me," Sam said, chuckling.

"I can think of better things to do on you, Detective." Just the sound of that husky voice in his ear was enough to get him going. *But not while driving…*

"Uh, yeah, about that, I guess it's too late for us to get together, uh, for a drink or something?"

"No, it's not too late. You wanna come over to my place?"

"Uh, yeah I'd like that, but it might be better if we met like in a bar or coffee place." Beads of sweat formed on Sam's forehead. "You know, get to know each other a little better before uh…"

"Doing the nasty?" Justin laughed that throaty laugh of his.

"Well, not exactly, but you know…"

"I didn't take you for a shy guy, Sam."

You have no idea. "Not shy really, just uh, careful, I guess."

"Okay, there's a wine bar in WeHo on the corner of Adams and Werner just off Melrose. It's open till eleven. You know it?"

"I'll find it. I'm pretty close to that area right now."

"Okay, give me about fifteen minutes and I'll meet you there."

"See you there." Sam relaxed a little now that he'd managed to divert the inevitable moment when he'd be alone with Justin. *God, you are an idiot, Walker. A grown man getting panicky by just imagining it.* But he'd never been any good with a one on one. Lack of self-esteem, his therapist had told him.

The irony was he craved it, longed for the contact, the affection that could come from it, but every time he got close to a man, kissed him—or started to anyway—he just dried up. Nothing happened down there. No excitement, no stirring of the blood. It used to drive Daryl up the wall. Shit, the fights they'd had about that.

'What is wrong with you?' Daryl had screamed at him.

'I don't know. It's not that I don't find you attractive. I do, I just don't know what causes this.'

But he did know. Liz thought that Daryl had done a number on him. He hadn't been the most supportive of boyfriends but the real reason for his lack of sexual drive had happened years before. He knew what the problem was—he just couldn't talk to Daryl about it. Nor did he want to relive what had happened to him. He was eighteen years old when just about the worst sexual experience anyone could ever have had been inflicted on him.

* * * *

'Hey, faggot!'

Sam had kept on walking away from the small hardware store he'd had a part-time job at. Since his father had thrown him out, he'd been staying at Kenny Murphy's house. Kenny's parents had been appalled when he'd told them what had happened. Kenny's dad had even called Sam's father, trying to make him see reason. He'd been cursed out for interfering and a visibly shaken Mr. Murphy had told Sam not to worry, he could stay as long as he needed to.

'Better you never go back to that house again.'

Sam had quickened his pace when he'd heard heavy running feet behind him. This hadn't been the first time he'd been singled out for a beating. Sam was no lightweight. At eighteen, his quarterback height and wide shoulders had been beginning to fill out and he'd exercised regularly. His dream had been to play for the NFL, but he hadn't been selected and now it looked like the police academy was a more viable choice.

The last time he'd been attacked, it had been by two bruisers, linebackers in one of the local school teams. He'd been fortunate that a police cruiser had happened by just as he'd been kicked to the ground. The creeps had taken off at the sound of the siren. He'd taken up more strength training since then and had felt confident he could take care of himself when necessary. He'd glanced behind him to see what he might be up against.

Four of them…shit. Two he could manage, three at a push, but four? *Hmm.* Well, he sure as hell wasn't going to run. They'd come at him all at the same time. He'd gone down under the sheer weight of four big bodies, his head hitting the sidewalk with a resounding crack and making him see stars. Before he could recover, he'd been dragged into an alley, stomped on, his clothes ripped from him, his jeans yanked down to his knees.

'*What the fuck are you doing?*' he'd screamed at them. The pain when they'd shoved whatever it was they were using up his ass had been excruciating. Their laughter had been like something out of a nightmare, high-pitched, out of control, almost inhuman. Sounds he'd known would haunt him for the rest of his life. They'd spat on him, pissed on him, rubbed his face in the alley filth. They'd left him there, most likely not caring if he lived or died.

In the hospital, he'd been treated for shock and various injuries both external and internal. The police had been amazingly sympathetic, but the four thugs had never been reprimanded. It was then that Sam had decided he had to leave Westhaven, Texas, and head for Los Angeles. Kenny and his mother had been against his leaving, but Sam had remembered Kenny's dad and the long look of understanding that told Sam he was doing the right thing.

* * * *

That had been a long time ago and sometimes he thought he was over it for the most part, but the memory of trauma such as he'd suffered never, in fact, went away.

Over the years he'd learned to live with it, thinking about it only in bleak times, except in the dreams he'd had no control over and which had haunted him almost every night for years. Sometimes they still did, even now that he was an adult, no longer a kid hurting both mentally and physically. The therapist had told him his lack of a sexual drive was only natural and in his opinion would improve as time went by. Perhaps if there had been someone there he could talk to, really talk to, it just might have helped. Not Daryl with his short-fuse temper.

Sometimes he still felt guilty about his and Daryl's relationship and the manner in which it had ended. Daryl had cheated, yes, but when he recalled the reasons Daryl had screamed at him, he could understand it in a way.

'You make me feel like I'm ugly, undesirable, worthless, and I can't live with that. So, I've been with someone else…so what? At least he can show me he wants me, not like you, staying limp every time I try to bring you pleasure. If I'd known you were going to lose interest so quickly I would never have agreed to move in with you…'

The pleasure I try to bring you… Sam sighed. Daryl's version of bringing him pleasure had been presenting his ass to Sam for a quick fuck with little or no foreplay. Kissing and caressing, the things that Sam craved, were rarely there. There was no rapport, no *warmth* between them. He'd wondered if the man Daryl left him for didn't care about such things.

He'd tried to express all this to the therapist, who seemed as uncomfortable as Sam was talking to the guy about not being able to maintain an erection, never minding getting it up in the first place. That was why he'd found it so amazing that he'd kissed Justin in the Blue Bar. He wasn't the type to start something he knew he couldn't finish. Yes, he'd been drunk, but he'd been drunk before and never laid one on a complete stranger, even a stranger as hot as Justin. And maybe it hadn't been such a bad kiss if Justin wanted to do it again.

The crazy element was Justin. This guy he'd never even met—well, not that he remembered with complete clarity—could get him going with the mere sound of his voice. How was that possible? He didn't want to jinx this. It already felt too good to be true, but maybe if they took it real slow he could psyche himself into thinking that he could really do it.

* * * *

The wine bar Justin had mentioned had an inviting atmosphere. Low lighting, some nice jazz piano in the background, candles on the tables and Justin sitting at one, smiling at him, and looking way better than the photo of him Sam had kept on his phone. He was wearing a light green polo shirt that might have been a size too small, the way it molded so perfectly across his chest. Still smiling, Justin patted the seat beside him.

"Hi there."

"Hi." Sam sat down awkwardly, knocking the table with his knee as he did so. "Sorry…clumsy."

"You seem nervous," Justin said. "I don't bite or anything, at least not in public."

Sam chuckled then looked up when a handsome guy approached their table and asked what he could bring them.

"I'd like a pinot noir, please," Justin said.

Wow, so polite. "I'll have the same, thanks." To Justin he said after the waiter left, "It's nice to really see you now that I'm completely sober. You must've thought I was a total slob the other night."

"I thought you were cute—sloppy, but cute." Sam grimaced and Justin chuckled. "Cute is kinda the wrong word for a guy who's big like you, but the expression on your face when you were trying so hard to form coherent sentences was really cute."

"Oh my God," Sam groaned. "And you actually wanted to see me again."

"The kiss is what did it. I'd never been kissed so *thoroughly* before in my life." He tilted his face toward Sam. "It was obvious you enjoy kissing. I'd like to think it was because it was me on the receiving end—and I can't wait for another one just like it."

Sam gripped the edge of the table to stop himself from diving on top of Justin and giving him what he'd just asked for. *That would go over well in here.* Justin's eyes widened as he seemed to understand Sam's intent.

"Your pinot noirs, sirs," the waiter announced, setting the glasses in front of them then pouring from the bottle balanced skillfully in his hand. Sam cleared his throat and paid attention while the waiter asked if there was anything else he could bring them. "A snack, perhaps? We have a nice selection. I can bring you a menu if you wish."

Justin flashed him a smile. "Nothing for me. How about you, Sam?"

"I'm good," Sam said, also smiling at the waiter.

"I bet you are," the waiter murmured and winked at Sam before taking off again.

"He totally flirted with you," Justin exclaimed. "There goes his tip."

Sam laughed. *The story of my life.* Dozens of guys flirted with him, but he reckoned he was probably the most sex-starved guy he knew.

"Not that I blame him." Justin gazed at him for a long moment. "You really are one helluva good-looking dude. How come you're single?"

"It's easier. I don't have to come up to anyone else's expectations."

"What does that mean?"

Sam sighed. "It means I'm a bad conversationalist and should be regaling you with lighthearted banter. You said you had a bad day and I'm not helping to make it better."

"Just being here with you makes it better."

Sam raised his glass. "Thanks, and thanks also for agreeing to meet me tonight."

Justin clinked his glass against Sam's and their eyes met. Justin's green eyes gleamed in the reflected light from the candle on the table and Sam's chest quickened. "So, I should ask you the same question, Justin. How come you don't have a boyfriend?"

Justin grimaced. "I used to, but it's a bit of a long story and not a pretty one. Maybe, like you, I've been thinking it's easier being single." His smile was like quicksilver in its return. "That's not to say I can't be tempted by the right man."

After they'd taken sips of the wine, he added, "I wish you'd agreed to come over to my place. I'd really like to kiss you right now."

Sam's gaze flitted to Justin's mouth. He loved the slight pout on Justin's lower lip. He got hard just imagining taking it between his teeth and nibbling lightly.

"I know what you're thinking," Justin said, all the tease in the world in his voice.

"Do you now?"

"Yes, and I know you're hard like me. Just looking at you does it for me, Sam."

Sam leaned back in his seat and smiled. *If only that was all there was to it.* "Something you should know before we get carried away imagining what we're gonna do when we're alone. You're right about me being hard right now. I've been hard off and on all day just thinking about you, but I have a problem and I don't want you to get disappointed when…well, if we ever have a chance of exploring, maybe, some more,"

"Exploring." Justin grinned. "I like the sound of that."

"I do too."

"So, let's finish our wine, pay the flirty waiter, go back to my place and do some exploring."

Despite his misgivings, Sam couldn't for the life of him ignore the sexy promise in Justin's smile. He nodded. "Okay."

* * * *

The cool night air on his face served to deflate Sam's ardor somewhat, but he didn't want to sound like a jerk by saying he'd changed his mind, so he walked with Justin to where their cars were parked.

Justin looked up at him. "You're taller than I remembered. I didn't get that from the other night."

"Was I on my hands and knees?"

"No!" Justin laughed and squeezed Sam's hand. "It's not very far, just stay close behind," he said, climbing into his Audi.

Sam nodded and did as directed, tailing Justin along Adams until he turned into a cul-de-sac then into a parking lot in front of a two-story apartment building. He was jittery and still in half a mind to tell Justin he had to go. He wanted this, but there was still 'the problem' and if it presented itself at the point of no return he would feel humiliated and Justin would no doubt be either pissed or understanding. Neither reaction would make him feel better. The latter might even make him feel worse.

Jesus, pull yourself together. Act like you look. Big and tough and able to take care of everything thrown at you. Well, that works good faced with criminals in dicey situations, not so much when alone with a sweet-looking guy like Justin. Oh shit.

He got out of his car and fixed a smile on his face as he walked toward the sweet-looking guy in question. Justin took his hand again and they entered the building together. In the elevator, Justin cast a worried glance at Sam.

"You okay? You seem antsy."

"No. I'm okay, really. Just, y'know, kinda nervous, maybe. I don't want you to be disappointed."

"Stop saying that. I know I won't be. It's gonna be great." The elevator door slid open and Justin, holding his hand, led him down a hallway long enough for Sam's nerves to accelerate into top gear.

He laughed. "You get a lot of exercise living here."

Justin tugged on his hand. "This is it." He unlocked the door and waved Sam in ahead of him.

Sam just about managed to say, "Nice place," before Justin had him up against the wall and was kissing the bejesus out of him. Sam crushed the slim body to his own and ground his crotch into Justin's. Their lips and tongues were working overtime, Justin apparently trying to overwhelm Sam's sensory capabilities. He pushed Sam's jacket aside and slid his hands under Sam's T-shirt, caressing his chest and fingering his nipples none too gently, causing Sam to groan into Justin's mouth and thrust his hips forward, gaining as much friction as he could against Justin's erection.

"Wow." Justin wrenched his lips from Sam's, his eyes sparkling. "I knew I wasn't dreaming about how great you kiss."

"Hey..." Sam was breathing heavily. "It takes two, you know—"

He didn't get further than that. Justin's lips were on Sam's again and the visceral glide of his tongue filled Sam with sensations he'd never in his life dreamed he would feel. The guy was, in a word, incredible, and even that didn't seem like a great enough word.

Justin dropped to his knees, taking Sam's zipper down with him, then unsnapping the waistband of his jeans. "Oh, man..." Justin lowered the elastic of Sam's boxer-briefs and held his erection at the base, gazing at it, a smile on his lips and a gleam in his eyes. "This is one beautiful cock, so long and thick...perfect," he murmured before licking up and down the pulsing length.

Sam gasped as the heat of Justin's mouth surrounded his cockhead then drew him in. He ran his fingers through Justin's curly hair and gave himself up to the ecstasy Justin's lips and tongue were bringing him. And *yes*—he was staying hard and it felt so good. Justin cupped his hands around Sam's ass cheeks and pulled him in tight, and Sam moaned. He was going to lose it any minute and he wanted this mind-blowing sensation to last...and last. It had been so long since it had felt this good and he wanted to howl at the moon. It was just that amazing.

Justin looked up at him and paused for just a moment to say, "Yeah, Sam, fuck my mouth. Want you." And Sam bucked his hips, ramming his cock into Justin's hot mouth. Justin took all of him, trapping him with his throat muscles clenched hard around the head of Sam's dick until Sam wanted to scream from the sheer carnal thrill of the climax that was building inside him.

"Justin. Oh my God, I'm gonna come, I'm gonna come!" Justin sucked harder and Sam bellowed like a bull, his orgasm overwhelming him in a series of mind-blowing jolts of ecstasy. When he'd got control he managed to gasp, "What about you?"

"You fucking me will take care of it."

"Bedroom?"

"To the left."

Sam picked Justin up with his arms around him and carried him into the bedroom. Their clothes were gone in an instant and Justin was stretched out on top of the bed, looking for all the world like sin personified, and Sam wasted no time. He dived onto Justin's throbbing cock, sucking it into his mouth and laving it with his tongue, eliciting moans and whimpers from the young designer.

"Oh yeah, Sam, that's it, you're so good, Sam."

Amazingly, Sam felt his erection returning. Had he found the cure for his E.D. in this beautiful young man? Had all Daryl's ministrations and curses and forcing him to take Viagra had the opposite effect, killing any chance of him getting hard enough to fuck him? The Viagra had sometimes worked, but he'd had the headache from hell afterward, nullifying all possible chance of enjoyment. But he didn't want to remember any of that right now. Right now, Justin was begging him to fuck him and he was up for that. Very much up for that.

"Condom?"

"And lube, top drawer." Justin pointed at the nightstand. He was smiling that incredible smile of his and for a moment Sam faltered, mesmerized by the guy's beauty. "Right there." Justin sounded impatient and Sam grinned. *Eager much?*

"Got it," he muttered and reached for the drawer. He knelt between Justin's legs while he squirted some lube onto his fingers then rubbed it over the rim around Justin's hole before inserting one long finger inside him. Justin squirmed and wrapped his arms around Sam's neck, pulling him down for a long, deep kiss.

"C'mon, my big butch cop," he whispered against Sam's lips when he'd released Sam from their kiss. He threw his legs up over Sam's shoulders and lifted his hips to give him clear access. "Fuck me till I can't sit down for a week."

What is it about this guy? Sam had never been so turned on. Justin was hot, without a doubt, but it was more than that. More than the thick eyebrows, the perfectly shaped nose and lips. It must be his eyes, so green and deep. It was like they could see inside him, into his screwed-up mind and soothe him, and at the same time make him hornier than he'd ever been in his life. Beads of sweat popped out on his forehead and his hands trembled when he slid the condom down his aching length. Justin gazed up at him through those incredible eyes filled with eager anticipation and Sam eased himself into the hot depths that awaited him.

He groaned as tight heat surrounded his pulsing cock and Justin pulled him down for another long, languorous kiss. The soft, wet glide of Justin's tongue over his did everything to increase Sam's lust. He pushed in then pulled out almost all the way before ramming himself back in, and Justin moaned into Sam's mouth and tightened his arms around Sam's hard torso. Sam squeezed a hand between them so he could reach Justin's cock and pump it to their quickening rhythm.

"Yes, give it to me, Sam," he groaned. "All the way, that's it, lover. Oh yeah…right there, Sam." And Sam, encouraged by Justin's obvious pleasure, gave it to him as hard and fast as he could. There was little refinement in their coupling, almost a desperation in their movements, but, oh, it was glorious. Sweat poured from his forehead and fell on Justin's lips and was immediately licked up and Justin's eyes held all the thrill and promise of the greatest fuck of Sam's life.

"Yes," he yelled and rammed in over and over until the dam burst and he almost blacked out from the overwhelming surge of his climax. Justin's body arched against him and he cried out when he came, his cum spilling over Sam's fingers and splattering over his chest.

"Oh my God, oh my God," Sam muttered through a heaving breath. He collapsed over Justin and held him in a crushing embrace, covering his face and throat and lips with searing-hot kisses, reveling in the fact that they were all returned with equal force.

"God, that was amazing," he whispered in Justin's ear, and the young man turned his face to Sam's and kissed him with a fervor that told Sam he agreed with him.

"You are the best," he murmured. "I may not be able to sit down for a week, just like I asked."

Sam chuckled. "Does that mean we can't do it again tonight?" He didn't want this incredible night to end…ever.

"Oh, we can do it again, over and over, as many times as you like. I've got lots and lots of lube."

They laughed together and held each other. Justin buried his face in the crook of Sam's shoulder, moving his lips over Sam's skin, flicking his tongue out to lick at the sweat.

"Mmm..." Justin clenched his ass muscles around the base of Sam's cock. "Don't slip out yet. I'm gonna feel really empty when you do."

Was it what Justin had just said or was it the lust that shone from his dark green eyes? Whatever it was, Sam experienced something he couldn't quite believe. He was growing hard again inside Justin, but he couldn't come again this quickly, could he? And especially not inside the same condom.

"Uh..."

"Wow." Justin gazed up at him, his beautiful eyes widening. "Sam, you're incredible. I can feel you getting hard again. You up for it? I am if you are."

"Yeah, but we'll need another condom."

"I'm on it. Why don't you...? Oh, you're out. Get rid of that one before you, you know, lose the inclination."

"Don't think there's much chance of that," Sam said, peeling the condom off his hardening cock. He tied it off then took it to the bathroom to dispose of it. Justin's admiring gaze zeroed in on Sam's erection as he climbed back into bed.

He wrapped his arms around Sam and kissed him. The sensations of Justin's warm lips and wicked, clever tongue were enough to have Sam coming way too soon. This was like nothing he'd ever known before. Justin had to have some kind of magical powers. Sam was convinced of it and laughed to himself at the idea. *Yeah, Sam, you're thirty years old and still believe in magic.* To be honest, he couldn't think of another explanation, other than magic, or maybe the simple fact that he and Justin were made for each other. That all it took to get over his E.D. was just meeting the right man.

Whatever, he was stupid to be thinking instead of doing and his aching cock was telling him so. He pushed

Justin's legs apart and knelt between them. Grabbing the lube, he got Justin ready for him, marveling that even after the thorough fucking he'd given him, Justin's ass was still tight and, if his wanton smile was anything to go by, he was still eager. He wasn't the only eager one and his fingers fumbled as he stretched the condom over his leaking cock.

Justin arched his body into Sam's first thrust, impaling himself on Sam's rigid length and throwing his arms around Sam's neck to pull him down for another one of the kisses they both loved so much.

It's in his kiss, he thought. The kiss he remembered now with such clarity. The one they'd shared in the bar, the one that had made Justin remember him and now, when he thought about it, something that might have just sealed their fate. Or was he hallucinating, getting so far ahead of himself that, if he wasn't careful, he might spoil everything by being over eager? But, *oh my God*, it felt as if Justin was right there with him, cleaving to Sam as he rammed into him.

He pushed into the kiss, his tongue tangling and tussling with Justin's and sending electric jolts of ecstasy from his lips to his cock to the soles of his feet. He'd never felt anything like this in his life. It *was* fucking magic!

Justin moaned into Sam's mouth, his hard cock gaining friction against Sam's torso. Sam reached between them and gripped it, pumping it to the steady rhythm of their bodies. They were cresting now. Sam could sure as hell feel it in his balls, but also in the way Justin's breath had quickened and the desperate way he clung to Sam.

"Sam!" Justin slammed up into him, his body taut as a bowstring, and he let loose a torrent of cum that coated both their chests with creamy heat. Sweat poured off Sam as he increased the pace of his hard thrusts. He was close, so close, and his orgasm when it came was like a dam bursting. He shook from the dizzying force of it, gasping out Justin's name before collapsing over him to be wrapped and held in Justin's arms.

They must have dozed off, because when Sam opened his eyes, Justin was snoring gently and Sam felt sticky and slightly gross. *Shit,* he still had the condom on. He eased away from Justin and padded into the bathroom to clean up. After he'd disposed of the condom, he used the washcloth he found hanging over the side of the sink to wipe off the dried cum and sweat, then rinsed it out and returned to the bedroom to tend to Justin. He was greeted with a murmured 'hi', a kiss and a muttered 'thanks' as he washed Justin's chest and stomach.

"You're beautiful," he said, brushing back the auburn curls from Justin's brow.

"And so are you." Justin smiled up at him. "Beautiful in a very butch way of course." He stroked Sam's chest. "Perfect muscles, not too much, just right, and I love that cleft in your chin." He punctuated his last remark with a kiss to Sam's chin.

Sam chuckled. "You do? It's a pain to shave around." He took Justin's hand and kissed it. "I have to tell you something."

Justin looked wary. "Oh, yeah?"

"For most of my life I've suffered from E.D.—until tonight, or rather until I met you, which, yeah, was only two nights ago, but when I started to remember you from the bar, how you looked, how you kissed, how you tasted, all of it gave me the hardest hard-on I've ever had in my life."

Justin stared at him, wide-eyed. "Are you kidding me? I can't imagine you with E.D. unless it stands for

Erectile Dynamite. Because that's what it felt like inside me. And when you did explode, the second time, I thought you were going to blow that condom to shreds."

"No, I didn't do that," Sam said right away, "just in case you were worried. I mean, I'm neg, but just to put your mind at ease."

"My mind is very much at ease, Detective." Justin grinned. "It's the rest of me that's wired. Just looking at you—wow. I can't really believe you're here with me." He reached up to stroke Sam's face. "Such pretty blue eyes." He ran his thumb over Sam's full lower lip and Sam sucked it into his mouth. "Oh…" Justin moaned. "That is so fucking sexy." He sat up, wound his arms around Sam and kissed him.

Sam sighed and opened to him, the warmth of Justin's tongue on his, his taste and scent firing Sam's senses once again. *What is happening?* he wondered. *What strange power does Justin have to bring me to the edge so quickly?* He gasped into Justin's mouth when the young man took Sam's hard-once-again cock in his hand and pumped it gently.

"You feel like you're ready for another round," Justin murmured on Sam's lips.

Sam was more than ready and didn't want to waste a minute of this amazing time spent with Justin. Justin must have dropped down from Heaven to bring him such rapture. All the years of suffering from an embarrassing lack of sexual spontaneity might just be behind him at last. He could only pray that this wasn't a one-night wonder. Shit, what if it was just the excitement of being with such a beautiful guy? He'd have to be made of ice not to be turned on by what, in Sam's opinion, was the perfect human. But right now, he was hard and ready to go just like Justin said.

"I am if you are." *Words I never thought I'd be able to say.*

"What do you think?" Justin gave him a teasing smile then pulled Sam down on top of himself.

Further conversation proved difficult when their mouths were full.

Chapter Five

Justin was surprised to find Paula waiting for him in his office the following morning. The euphoria he'd been enjoying since his evening of amazing sex with Sam was quickly dispelled by the expression on her face.

"Good morning," he said, trying to smile. "You look a tad grim." He started to hang his laptop satchel on the coatrack but stalled when Paula sighed.

"She sent me to do her dirty work," Paula told him.

Justin's shoulders slumped. "She's firing me."

Paula nodded. "She says you were rude and insubordinate and regardless of how talented you think you are—her words not mine—she is not prepared to overlook your rudeness or your obvious disregard for her authority." She paused and gave Justin a sympathetic look. "I'm really sorry, Justin. As far as I'm concerned, you've been a major asset to the company and I think she's making a big mistake."

"So do I, but that's her problem not mine." Justin shrugged. "Something's been up her ass for the past few days. It's not just me she's been sniping at. I've heard her saying some pretty rough things to you and two of the seamstresses were in tears yesterday. Do you know what's going on?"

"She and her husband have been fighting for over a month and she kicked him out last week."

"So we all have to suffer because of her bad marriage? What a crock. Fucking unprofessional, if you ask me."

"But no one's asking you, Justin!" The steely, accented voice behind him made him curse under his breath. She'd snuck up on them like she loved to do from time to time. The woman was a lousy boss in his opinion and he wasn't about to retract his 'unprofessional' comment.

"Come to wish me *hasta la vista*, Maria?"

"I've come to tell you I want those latest designs you did. The ones in your laptop. Upload them to my computer before you leave."

"Not on your life, lady." Justin hefted the satchel onto his shoulder. "These designs are mine. Done on my own time and they go with me. You see fit to fire my ass, I take what is mine."

"I will sue you, you ingrate," Maria yelled.

"Bite me." He turned to Paula. "It was nice working with you, Paula. Sorry you'll still have to put up with the crap that flies around here on a daily basis." He fixed Maria with a threatening look. "And don't even try to withhold my last paycheck or I'll be suing *you*."

"Get out!"

"With pleasure. Good luck finding someone to take my place."

He strode out of the office and took the elevator down to the garage. *Well, this is a pisser,* he thought as he climbed into his car. Mentally he tried to work out how long he could remain unemployed without having to give up his apartment. First thing, he had to send out his resume and find another job, *asap*!

* * * *

Sam found a quiet spot in the hall outside the office to call Justin later that day. "How's it goin'?"

"Hey." Justin sounded down. "Crap day, I'm afraid. Cruella De Vil fired me for being rude and insubordinate, she said."

"Wow, sorry."

"And the bitch wanted me to leave my designs behind."

"Could she claim she was paying you to draw the designs?"

"She can claim all she wants," Justin snarled. "These I did on my own time in my own apartment. How late are you working?"

"Late. We're following some info on a case we're working on."

"Oh. It'll sound whiny, but I really could use your big strong arms around me right now."

"Sorry, Justin."

"I know, I know. I've known you for all of four days. Bit early to start making demands upon your person."

Sam laughed. "When I'm off-duty, you can make all the demands you want upon my person."

"Mmm, I like the sound of that. Thank you for last night, by the way…it was fantastic."

"Yeah, it was." He wanted to say 'best ever', but that might be too much so early on in their friendship. "I think I should be thanking you for helping me get over, you know, what I told you about."

A smile was in Justin's voice when he said, "I was only too happy to help. I can still feel you up there...must've been the third or fourth time that did it."

Oh, wow. His cock pulsed in his briefs. Any more of this kind of talk and he was going to have to head for the men's room. Clearing his throat, he asked, "Do you have any leads for another job?"

Justin laughed lightly, as though he knew Sam's dilemma. "I've been online putting out my resume all over the place, so something'll pop sooner or later. In the meantime, my mother's been buggin' me to come visit the old folks at home, so I'm gonna take a couple of days and do just that."

"Where do they live?"

"Kansas. Ugh, I know, not a friendly place for gay boys and girls, but my folks have always been supportive about my being gay, so I don't mind going back now and then."

"Nice that you have good parents supporting you."

"Yeah, they're the best really. How 'bout you? Your parents still around?"

"I wouldn't know, and— Gotta go, Justin. I'll call you later. Bye."

"Bye."

Justin put his phone away and frowned. *'I wouldn't know, and...'* What was he going to say? *'And mind your own business,' or 'and I don't wanna talk about it' or 'and I don't give a shit'?* So many things he didn't know about Detective Sam Walker. Somewhere in his life, things must've gotten screwed up. He could sense that behind the rough-tough-cop exterior was a vulnerable man, unsure of his own capabilities.

'I just don't want you to be disappointed,' he'd said in the elevator. *Why would he have thought I'd be disappointed? The man is a powerhouse in bed.* And that thing about the E.D? That was weird. And yet he wouldn't have just made it up. That was definitely not the kind of thing most men bragged about. Maybe he could coax more about it out of him when next they met, whenever that might be. Sounded like the case he was on was going to take some time to solve.

Well, now that I'm a man of leisure I better call Mom and give her the good news that I'll be visiting for a few days.

* * * *

When Sam and Martin checked in at the precinct the following day the captain called them into his office. "Listen, Sam, you and Martin try and wrap up the murdered hustler case quick as you can, okay?"

"Captain, we've only had it two days," Martin exclaimed.

"I know, but this is not deemed a high priority case, if you catch my drift. I don't agree with my superiors, but you know how it goes. I don't want this to become another cold case."

"Right, Captain." Sam glanced at Martin as they walked back to their desks. Martin was scowling at him big-time. "I know what you're thinking, but there's no use getting in the captain's face about it."

"Makes me so goddamned mad, Sam. A murdered kid isn't considered high priority. Just because of what he was, of course. Dispensable 'cause he doesn't fit the norm. If he was a high school grad, it would be a whole different story. I mean, have you even seen a newspaper report on this case?"

"I know, I know, it stinks." Sam was as pissed as his partner, but it wasn't the first time they'd seen cases like this swept away under pressure. Joey Carter's cold, lifeless form lying in the morgue was all that remained of the once 'sweet and crazy' kid. That was how the young hustler, Rolando, had described him. *Damn this world and the misery it can sometimes bring.*

George Mackie and his partner, Eliot Sanders, sauntered into the room. Mackie tipped his head in their direction, but Sanders averted his eyes from Sam's. *Yeah, thought so. Pretty sure you're the one who bad-mouthed me the other day. Never liked you anyway.*

"Afternoon, guys," Martin sang out. Mackie returned his greeting, but Sanders stayed silent. "I said, 'Afternoon', *De*tective Sanders. What, you're too good to say it back to your fellow detectives?" Sanders continued to ignore Martin, turning on his computer and staring at the screen instead. "Fuck me," Martin muttered under his breath.

"Leave it," Sam said, but he should've known Martin wasn't one to ignore a challenge.

"What? You got your wrist slapped yesterday for calling a fellow officer a fag?" Martin chuckled. "Ya think we didn't know it was you just because you didn't 'fess up? Moron. Try it again and I'll insist on suspension—after I lay you out."

"Martin, sit, so we can discuss our next move." Sam rolled Martin's chair over to his desk. "Sit."

"Motherfucker," Martin muttered, sitting anyway. "You should make a formal complaint."

"What's the point? LAPD can do all the sensitivity training they want, but you can't change hearts and minds where there are none."

"There is that. The creep just riles me up."

Sam chuckled. "That's not to say that if I should come upon him in a dark alley, I wouldn't punch him on the nose."

Martin's teeth gleamed against his dark skin as a huge grin spread across his face. "Now that's more like it, partner!"

"Anyway, we have enough to think about, especially after the captain warned us about wrapping things up quick as we can."

"Right," Martin grumped. "Still pisses me off. Let's go get some lunch. The air in this place stinks today." Martin swung around on his chair and glared across at Sanders. "Damned putrid, if you ask me. Right, Sam?" He jumped to his feet and headed for the door.

Chuckling, Sam followed.

* * * *

Justin sat on a bench in his sister's backyard, watching while Simon, his three-year old nephew, played ball with his dad.

"Kevin, not so hard," Jen called out. "He's only got little hands."

Justin chuckled under his breath. There had been a time when he'd hoped Kevin would get 'hard' with him. His doctor bro-in-law was a cutie and, even after six years of marriage and his sister's excellent cooking, had kept his toned physique. Not a patch on Sam, of course, but Jen was a lucky, lucky girl to have such a hot husband.

Kevin signaled that he'd heard her and she leaned in closer to Justin. "So, who are you seeing these days and when do we get to meet him?"

Justin laughed. "I am seeing someone, matter of fact, but I met him only four days ago, so no way am I asking him to come meet the folks, and you."

"Is he hot?"

"Of course. You think I'd waste my valuable time on some dweeb?"

She shoved his arm. "You are so conceited. Does he know what he's in for?"

"I think so," he said with a mischievous smile. "He's a cop, and he's kinda deep, like there's a lot going on in his mind. I see myself as someone to cheer him when he's blue, make him smile, help him forget the nasties he has to deal with. He and his partner just broke a case involving a child-slave ring. Can you imagine what kind of creeps would do a heinous thing like that?"

"No, I can't," Jen said, her gaze immediately zeroing in on little Simon. She shuddered. "God, why would anyone want to put a little kid through that kind of horror?"

Simon chose that moment to charge across the lawn, jump onto Justin's lap and wrap his arms around Justin's neck, raining sloppy kisses on his face.

Justin laughed. "Hey, you supply towels with those kisses?"

"Amazing," Jen said. "He hasn't seen you in almost in six months and he's loving on you right away. He sees Michael every other week and never shows him the same kind of attention."

"Well, consider the source. Michael is the biggest ass…I mean grumpy-pants in all of Kansas, isn't he, Simon, isn't he?" He jumped to his feet and swung Simon around, eliciting screams of laughter from his nephew.

"Justin!" Jen pretended to look annoyed. "You know he'll say 'grumpy pants' right at Michael next time he's here, don't you?"

"Yes, all the better to get up his nose." He stopped swinging Simon about. "He's not on his way over, is he?" he asked with mock terror.

"No, thank goodness." Kevin's deep voice sounded close to Justin's ear as he put his arm around Justin's shoulders. Simon tried to cuddle them both at the same time but couldn't get his short arms around both Justin and Kevin's necks. "Come here, you little tyke," Kevin crooned, lifting him off Justin. "So, what were you two talking about or should I not know?"

"Justin's dating a cop," Jen said smugly.

"Really?" Kevin gaped at him. "There are such people?"

"What, cops?"

"*Gay* cops. What is the world a'comin' too, huh, Simon?"

They all laughed and Justin was suddenly very glad to be home. He loved his family. Well, all except Michael, who really was an asshole, but Jen and Kevin and his mom and dad and little Simon, of course, he wouldn't trade for any number of millions of dollars.

His cell buzzed and he hastily pulled it from his pants pocket. *Sam, maybe, I hope? No, Maria. What the fuck does she want? She is not getting those designs, unless of course she wants to pay handsomely for them.* He chuckled when he pressed the Speak button. *I can be bought just like anyone else.*

"Hi, Maria. What can I do for you?"

"Oh, Justin, I think perhaps I spoke and acted too hastily yesterday. Paula made me see that Esteban

Fashions has benefitted greatly from your presence." There was a long pause.

She's hating this, Justin thought, grinning at Jen, who was staring at him with raised eyebrows. *Maria,* he mouthed at her.

"Anyway," Maria continued, her voice sounding as if she were talking through clenched teeth, "would you consider rejoining Esteban?"

"Well, I hadn't really officially left," Justin said sweetly, "as no severance has been signed and no final paycheck delivered so I guess we could just pick up where we left off…without the shouting, of course."

"*Of course*. So, I can expect to see you tomorrow?"

"Not tomorrow. I had no plans for the next few days after you fired me, so I flew up to visit my folks. I can be there Monday if that's okay with you."

"Yes, that's fine," Maria snapped. "Monday then, and be sure to bring your latest designs with you. I want to see them."

"Of course, Maria." Justin bit back the laugh that was threatening to burst from him. "See you Monday morning. Bye." He shut his phone off. "Oh, that must have killed her to give me my job back."

"She did, already?" Kevin frowned. "Fires you one day, wants you back the next. Sounds like she's a flake to me."

"Among other things."

"But it's good you have your job back," Jen said. "Mom can stop worrying about you."

Kevin chuckled. "But she won't. She lives to worry about her baby boy."

"Smart aaaa—" He caught himself in time as Simon gave him a gap-toothed grin. "Arthur."

Kevin chortled. "Smart Arthur?"

"I think it's time we ate," Jen said, rolling her eyes. "Fancy a glass of wine, Justin? I picked up a really nice and fruity Chardonnay at the market. It'll go well with the chicken dish we're having for dinner."

"Sounds delicious," Justin said as they walked back to the house.

"So what's he like, this gay cop of yours?" Kevin asked, nudging Justin's arm. "Should I be jealous?"

Justin chuckled. "Very jealous. He's great, but like I told Jen, we met just four days ago so who knows where it'll go. He's on a new case right now and he thinks it's gonna take a lot of night-time work, so…"

"Well, good luck. I hope it works out," Kevin said. "You need a guy in your life. Somebody stable, unlike that asswipe Brad…ugh. I can't be there for you all the time you know." They laughed, their heads close together, and Justin kissed Kevin's cheek.

"You're my favorite brother-in-law."

"I'm your *only* brother-in-law, so I'm supposed to be over the moon with this compliment?"

"You two…" Jen shook her head at them. "Just as well I know my husband is as straight as…as straight as—"

"An arrow?" Justin suggested.

"That's it, oh, and I love that show on the CW."

"That's settled then." Kevin winked at Justin. "How about that, then, Simon? Your dad's as straight as an arrow on TV."

Simon gurgled his agreement.

The doorbell ringing announced the arrival of Jen and Justin's mom and dad and an end to the silliness. Kevin took Simon to the door so the parents could make a fuss of him and, from the shrieks and exclamations, they were doing just that.

* * * *

Later, alone in the guest room, Justin texted Sam and got an immediate response when his cell buzzed.

"Hi, I thought you might be too busy for talking."

"It's been a shit day, but the sound of your voice makes it better."

Justin chuckled. "You say the nicest things, Detective. So, any luck on the new case?"

"Couple of leads, but not enough for my liking. Are you having a good time with your family?"

"Yes…can't help but think though I'd rather be spending time with you, getting to know you better."

"I'd like that too." A pause. "Are you in bed?"

"Getting there. How about you?"

"I'm still at the precinct. Martin and I are going over what we learned today. He just went to the restroom."

"So, no phone sex then?" Justin laughed at the startled noise Sam made on his end. "Shock you, Detective?"

"Yes! And now I'm gonna have to hang up 'cause you've made me all… Shit, here's Martin. I'll call you tomorrow. Bye."

Justin was still laughing when he turned off his cell.

Oh my big, shy and handsome detective. What I'm going to do to you when next we have time together. I cannot wait!

Chapter Six

Sam and Martin sat in their car, watching the action in the park from a fairly well-hidden vantage point. It was a cloudy night, the moon making only brief appearances in between breaks in the clouds. The tall trees on their side of the park cast long shadows over the scrubby grass and Sam could see the occasional glow of a cigarette in the dark.

Sam nodded, his eyes trained on a movement near the center of the park. He opened the glove compartment and pulled out a pair of binoculars. The moon breaking through helped while he adjusted the vision. "Fuck me," he breathed.

"What?" Martin stared out the window.

"It's Sanders. What the hell is he doing out there?"

"Gimme those." Martin snatched the binoculars from Sam and squinted through them at the figure wearing a long black trench coat. "You're right. Sanders, and he's…oh shit, he's talkin' to some kid, giving him something. Now they're walkin' off toward those trees. Man, I cannot believe this. Even scum like Sanders."

"The kids said some of their johns were cops," Sam said, seething. "Let's go." He was out of the car and heading for the trees before Martin could ease himself from behind the steering wheel. Sam pounded across the park, cursing as a car engine started up. He ran out onto the road in time to see a black SUV driving toward Santa Monica Boulevard. He strained to catch the license number but the light over the plate was out.

"Damn," he muttered. Martin joined him, puffing out big breaths. "The son of a bitch was prepared. Probably had a driver waiting."

"How the hell is he going to explain this away?" Martin rasped, still trying to catch his breath. "Man, but I have to get in shape."

"He can't. Sorry, Martin, we have to get back to the car. Let's go."

"Oh, *man*."

"Traffic's always bad on Santa Monica," Sam said, "so we have a chance of catching up, or at least keeping him in our sights. See where he's going."

"Yeah, yeah, you drive"—he threw Sam the keys—"while I give myself some CPR."

They got a break at the end of the road. There was no left turn onto Santa Monica so they didn't have to toss up which way to go. "Keep an eye out for a black SUV up ahead," Sam said.

"Right, 'cause there's hardly any of those."

Sam chuckled and punched in the precinct's number. "Hi, Mary, get me the duty sergeant please. Thanks. Hey, Captain Thomason, got a problem here. The area McCready and I are staking out for the case. Yeah, that one. Detective Sanders just approached a kid in the park and drove off with him in a black SUV, don't have the make yet. You have a take on this? Didn't think so. Okay, we're on Santa Monica Boulevard heading west. I'll call in again when we get a fix on the vehicle."

"There it is," Martin said. "Turning left at the light."

"Roger that." He turned left, leaving enough room so that Sanders wouldn't get antsy. The SUV made several turns into a residential area then pulled up onto a driveway and stopped. Sam parked behind it, barring the exit.

"Hey, Sanders," Martin yelled when the occupants got out. Eliot Sanders and his partner, George Mackie, and a young guy in his teens.

Sanders glared at them. "What d'you guys want?"

"You wanna explain this?" Sam asked him. "We watched you approach this kid in the park and drive away with him. What gives?"

"What the fuck business is it of yours?"

"We were staking out the park, dumbass," Martin snapped. "Don't you know what's going on in your own precinct? You heard Hoskins give us the case of the murdered hustler. You waltzed into the middle of our stakeout and drove away with a kid. What do you think we're gonna think?"

"Oh wow…" The kid grinned at Sanders. "You really messed up, Uncle El."

Mackie groaned and Sanders began to sputter. "I—I didn't know. His mother said he'd gone out to meet friends and he got lost. Went to the wrong park, I guess."

"Is this true, son?" Sam asked.

"Yeah, kinda."

"What does that mean, *kinda*?" Martin snapped

"I didn't get lost. My friends sent me to that fag park on purpose just to razz me."

"*Fag park*?" Martin growled.

"Yeah, where all those queers hang out. We were fixin' to beat some of them up, but I guess my buds chickened out."

"Oh, I see..." Martin fixed Sanders with an evil eye. "Like uncle, like nephew, huh? Teaching him early about who to hate. Who to pick on. Good one, Sanders. Be proud of yourself."

The kid sneered. "What, are you guys fags, too? I thought you were cops."

"Shut up, Kirby," Sanders snapped. "That's enough!"

"Kirby?" Martin chortled. "Better get a *grip*, kid."

"Martin, let's go." Sam turned on his heel. "We have to call this in." He was having a hard time not busting out laughing at the expressions on Sanders' and his nephew's faces. *Talk about dumb and dumber*. Yeah, he and Martin had made a wrong call, but what in hell was Sanders thinking being okay with his punk of a nephew going into West Hollywood to beat up on hustlers? *What a scumbag.*

"Oh, my good *God,*" Martin groaned as he piled into the car. "What a bunch of assholes. Can you believe those guys? If I was Mackie, I'd ask for a new partner. Jeez!" He bumped Sam's shoulder. "I guess it was too much to hope Sanders really was mixed up in this mess. I so want to deck that jerk."

"You'll have to stand in line behind me," Sam said. "Okay, let me call this in before Thomason puts out an APB on Sanders."

* * * *

Justin was not happy when he got home. He'd had a great weekend regardless of the fact it had been Sam-less, but fortunately it had also been Michael-less. He'd kept his fingers crossed that his big brother wouldn't show with his usual display of homophobia and tactless comments about little Simon's fondness for his Uncle Justin.

They had almost come to blows on one of Justin's visits home and it had ended up with his dad throwing Michael out—until he decided to apologize, which of course didn't happen. Justin hadn't seen his brother since then and he was happy to keep it that way.

So the weekend had gone seamlessly with everyone getting on like a house on fire and enjoying once another's company. Justin's only gripe was that he wasn't spending at least a part of it with Sam. Seamlessly, that was, until the return flight got screwed up and delayed by more than three hours so that he missed his connection and arrived in LAX after midnight. At least his car was in the parking lot and he didn't have to wait for a cab or Uber amid the seething masses of grouchy passengers.

Then, of course, dealing with the 405 didn't help. He was always amazed that there weren't more accidents on that freeway as even at almost one a.m. the traffic was shitty, to say the least. All this and the fact he'd decided to get to work early so he could secure his boss' newfound liking for his work.

No sooner was he through the door than his cell chimed. Seeing Sam's name on the screen rid him of his grouchiness in an instant.

"Hi, Sam, how are you?"

"Okay. Sorry to call so late. I thought I might have to leave a message. Are you home?"

"Just walked in the door. Where are you?"

"Leaving the precinct. How about if I—"

"That'd be great. Come on over."

Sam's chuckle was sexy, like the rest of him. "How did you know what I was going to ask?"

"I didn't know, just hoped." Justin also hoped he wasn't being too gushy.

"I'll see you in about ten minutes, okay?"

"Very okay."

After they'd hung up, Justin flew into the shower and made sure every nook and cranny was clean as a whistle. His earlier fatigue and surliness were gone. Amazing what the prospect of seeing a special man could do for him. He was quick drying himself and wondered if Sam would like a drink, or maybe even a shower. *Shit.* He should've waited, then they could have showered together. The thought of that, of Sam's hunky body all wet and soapy, sliding over his. *Oh man, don't get all hot and bothered already. Take it easy.* Still what was wrong with showing him just how happy he was about this unexpected visit?

He pulled a pair of sweat shorts and a T-shirt from his dresser drawer then ran his hands through his still damp curls. Sam would know he'd just showered. Too much pressure or would he be happy Justin had gone to the trouble? No, it wasn't any trouble. Shit, he was going giddy with nerves. *Calm down, he'll be here in a minute or so and doesn't want to see some jittery queen.*

The doorbell chiming made him jump. *Get a fucking grip! What the fuck, I'm gonna show him I'm happy to see him!*

He ran to the door and yanked it open, a great big smile on his face. Sam blinked. "Wow, I've never been greeted like this before. How are you, Justin?"

"Better. Now you're here." He pulled Sam inside and wrapped his arms around him, looking for a kiss. Sam didn't disappoint him. Their mouths came together with almost painful force, tongues meshing together in a pouring-out of passion that had Justin seeing stars. Their breath filled each other's mouths. Soft moans and whimpers vibrated on their lips while their arms tightened around each other's bodies. It seemed as if there was no closeness close enough for either of them.

"God," Justin croaked when at last they broke the kiss and slackened their holds on each other. "I knew I'd missed you, but I didn't realize how much until I saw you standing there in all your hunky glory."

Sam laughed. "I missed you too. I just hope you had a much better weekend than I did."

"It was good. Hey, can I get you something to drink?"

"Would you mind if I used your shower? You smell so nice and I'm kinda rank from sitting in the car for hours."

"Help yourself. I'll get you a fresh towel." Justin kicked himself mentally. He should have waited on that shower. Then he could've suggested that they shower together. *Doofus.*

By the time he brought the towel to the bathroom, Sam was already in the shower and Justin leaned against the vanity, enjoying the view of Sam's big, well-formed body which he could see outlined through the steamy glass.

"Are you peeking?" Sam asked, chuckling.

"Yes. I admit to having no shame. I'd never pass up the opportunity to ogle a beautiful man's body."

Sam snorted. "Beautiful?"

"Beauty is in the eye of the beholder, you know, and—" He gasped when Sam slid the shower door open then stepped out. "And beauty is what I'm beholding right now."

"You have quite the silver tongue, Justin," Sam said as he accepted the towel Justin handed him.

"And I know just what to do with it."

Sam smiled and pulled Justin into his arms. "Give me that tongue," he murmured, touching his parted lips to Justin's. The kiss was long and sweet and Justin smoothed his hands down the length of Sam's muscular back then farther to cup and squeeze the twin globes of his ass. He squeaked when Sam upended him over his shoulder and carried him into the bedroom.

"Put me down, varlet," he said through his laughter, slapping Sam's butt.

Sam dumped him on the bed then pulled his shorts and T-shirt off. Justin's hard cock sprang out and Sam licked it from base to tip before taking it into his hand and mouth, sucking and squeezing until Justin thought he might pass out from the inability to breathe. He ran his fingers through Sam's short dark hair, caressed the sides of his face, his ears, his neck, and Sam hummed his appreciation, the vibration sending chills and thrills through Justin's entire body.

He yelped when Sam flipped him over, kissed him from his nape to his tailbone then nibbled on each rounded cheek, making Justin writhe and buck and moan.

"The first time I saw your beautiful ass," Sam said in between licks and nibbles, "I knew I had to taste it. And it's delicious, just like I knew it would be."

Sam slipped his tongue into the hot recess of Justin's ass, circling and teasing the rim with the tip of his tongue and driving Justin wild. When he plunged his tongue inside him, Justin almost came off the bed. Sam gripped Justin's hips, holding him in place while he rimmed him, and Justin sank into the pleasure washing over and through him, moaning Sam's name over and over.

Sam reached between Justin's legs and gripped his pulsing shaft. Justin cried out. The ecstasy was almost too much, coming at him, it seemed, from so many pleasure points at once. Now Sam added a finger alongside his tongue and found that sweet spot that had Justin coming apart. Justin reared up, pressed himself into Sam's chest, snaked an arm around Sam's neck and pulled him in for a searing kiss, a choking plea carried on hot breath. "Fuck me, Sam. Oh, please, fuck me."

Sam kissed Justin's neck then turned him around onto his back. He grabbed the lube and condom, got himself ready then raised Justin's legs to give himself access to Justin's eager hole. He pressed forward, gasping as Justin's heat and inner muscles drew him in. He moved slowly at first, letting Justin adjust to the pressure, but from the look of sheer wanton abandon on Justin's face, perhaps he was way ahead of him.

Sam reveled in the fact that they fit together so well. Once again his fears of disappointing Justin diminished and he gave himself up to the very real pleasure that having sex with Justin brought him.

Justin smiled up at him and Sam's heart turned over. This was so perfect. Justin was perfect. Sam leaned in for another of the amazing kisses they shared and while pleasure flowed through him, he allowed just the tiniest bud of hope to lodge in his heart that this could be something more than just sex.

He moved inside Justin, long, thrusting strokes that brought him closer and closer to the edge and Justin moaned and arched upward as Sam bore down. Justin took his erection in his hand and began pumping it in time to Sam's increasing momentum. The vision of Justin under him, the look of concentration on his beautiful face and the glide of his rigid cock through his fist were the most erotic things Sam had ever seen.

Justin gasped, his chest heaved, his eyes met Sam's and he cried out Sam's name when he climaxed, his hot cum spraying over both of them. Sam couldn't hold back another second. The force of his orgasm caused his body to arch back and up and he brought Justin with him, their bodies clamped together in an all-consuming embrace as every vestige of cum was wrung from Sam, leaving him sated and exhilarated beyond anything he'd ever known before.

Sam held Justin pressed to him while he rained kisses on his mouth and throat. The words *I love you* danced in his mind and it took all his willpower to stop himself from saying them out loud. It was too soon and he didn't want to freak Justin out and spoil what they had, what they perhaps might have in the future.

"What're you thinking about?" Justin stroked Sam's cheek and kissed him gently. "You always seem to be lost in thought."

"They're good thoughts when I'm with you," Sam said, returning Justin's kiss. "It's just that sometimes I feel this is all too good to be true. My being able to perform, I mean."

"And *perform,* as you put it, like a stallion." Justin chuckled. "Not that I've ever had a stallion, you understand, but maybe how I imagine it would be."

"You're amazing," Sam said. "You make me smile even when I'm not with you. Just the thought of you is enough. Not to mention what you do to my libido. No one has ever done that for me before." He raised himself onto his elbow and gazed at Justin for a long moment before he said, "I should tell you something that maybe will help you to understand what I'm talking about."

"Okay, but only if you want to." Justin ran his thumb over Sam's lower lip. "I know there are things that are not always easy to share."

Sam sucked Justin's thumb for a second or two before replying. "You're right, but I think you should hear this because…well, you've made a huge difference in my life. I know sex isn't the be all and end all of a relationship, but it is important. My last partner left me because I couldn't satisfy him, and some of that was definitely my fault. I had convinced myself I would have E.D. for the rest of my life after what happened when I was much younger. But then I met you." He paused to kiss Justin on the lips. "And I am very glad you didn't give me the brush-off when I came on to you in my drunken state."

Justin kissed him back. "You and me both."

Chapter Seven

"So tell me what happened when you were younger."

Sam leaned back on the pillow, slipped an arm under Justin's shoulders and Justin laid his head on Sam's chest.

"You really want to hear about all that?" Sam asked, running his fingers through Justin's curls.

"Most definitely." Justin looked up into Sam's eyes. "I want to know everything about you."

"I was eighteen, almost out of high school, working part time in a hardware store and tossing up between enlisting or applying for the police academy. Anyway, the night it happened I'd just locked up the store when four yahoos jumped me. I was pretty fit, even then, but there were just too many of them and when I went down I hit my head real hard on the sidewalk. They dragged me into an alley. They were saying all kinds of crap, calling me a faggot, saying I'd disgraced my family, that I deserved to die, they were going to cut off my balls. All kinds of shit. Then...well, shit, I don't know if I can tell you this."

"What did they do to you, Sam? I want to know so I can hate them even more than I do now."

"They…they shoved a metal rod inside me."

Justin stared at Sam in horror. "Oh, my God, Sam…that's…that's…"

"Awful, yeah. Hard to find words for that kind of creepy stuff."

"But, Sam, you could've died!"

"Nearly did. I never knew it was possible to lose so much blood as I did that night. I managed to crawl back out of the alley and a guy walking his dog saw me and called 9-1-1. They stitched me up, I got blood transfusions and antibiotics and fortunately the infection I could've gotten from the rust on the metal didn't take hold and cleared up pretty fast."

"Oh, God, Sam. I just can't imagine anything so terrible." His expression changed from sadness to anger. "I hope they got the fuckers that did it."

"Nope, never did. I didn't know them, couldn't even give a decent description, they hit me so fast."

"Your folks must have been devastated."

"Not really."

"What d'you mean, *not really*?"

Sam sighed. This was the part of his past he rarely talked about.

"Sam!" He could tell Justin wasn't about to let it go unanswered. "Sam, don't tell me they didn't care about what had happened?"

"They never knew about it. At least, I didn't tell them. And as far as I know no one else did either. They disowned me when I came out to them, and my buddy's folks took me in."

"Jesus, Sam." Justin's eyes filled with tears. "I am so sorry."

"It's okay." He stroked Justin's face gently. "It was a long time ago and I'm over it really."

"No, you're not. How could you be? All these terrible things happening to you? Oh, Sam…" He lay on top of him and kissed his lips and throat. "Sam, Sam," he crooned. "I wish I could make you forget. I can't but let me help you make it better, if only for a little while."

"I didn't mean to turn this into a pity party," Sam said. "I just wanted to let you know what caused the E.D. and how much you have done to end it…to make me whole."

"And I'm not doing this out of pity." Justin straddled Sam's thighs. "I'm doing this because in a very short space of time you've become my hero."

Sam chuckled. "Me?"

"Yes, you. I don't think you realize just what a great guy you are. Well…" He lowered his head to kiss Sam's chest. "I'm gonna remind you of that fact every chance I get," he added before trailing his lips up to Sam's mouth.

Sam sighed into their kiss. The feel of Justin's warm, lithe body pressed to his was like a balm to his very soul.

* * * *

Justin wasn't particularly looking forward to going back to work at Esteban Fashions, but it was a job, after all, and until he could find one where he'd feel more appreciated, it would have to do. He just hoped Maria wasn't in one of her bitchy moods. He often wondered how Paula had put up with her continual carping over the years she'd worked for her. It had to be galling to not only listen to Maria complaining about the employees and their terrible standard of work but of Paula's own lack of drive and unwillingness to discipline the staff.

All that was in Maria's mind only, and Justin didn't doubt for a second that she added, 'especially Justin' to the lack of discipline complaint. *She must be one unhappy woman…and hell to live with, I bet.*

He could of course block all of this out by reliving the wonderful hours he'd spent with Sam last night. Up until the moment he'd had to leave so quickly, anyway. He wondered if Sam was as woozy from lack of sleep as Justin was this morning. *No, bet he's not.* He'd also bet that Sam 'on the job' was a power to be reckoned with, just as he was in bed.

God, that story he'd told him last night… unbelievable. Only he did believe it, and when he'd called Sam his hero, he'd meant it from the heart. The sex they'd had after Sam's revelation had been truly fantastic. What Justin found unbelievable was Sam's insistence that it was all because of him…Justin. He'd love to take credit, but it was so easy to show how much he enjoyed making love to Sam. He couldn't imagine anyone thinking otherwise. Whoever Sam had felt he'd disappointed in the past must have had their own hang-ups.

That night, a week ago, in the bar, Justin had gazed into Sam's eyes and felt his heart turn over, and now each time they met, which, as far as Justin was concerned, wasn't nearly frequent enough, he felt himself being drawn closer and closer to the hot detective.

If Sam thinks that I'm responsible for his prowess between the sheets, then that's fine with me. I just hope he lets me prove it again and again.

The quiet chuckle that slipped from his lips was cut short by the sharp buzz of the intercom on his desk.

"Justin?"

Who else? "Yes, Maria."

"Come into my office, please."

"Right away."

Groaning, he rose from his desk and marched smartly down the hall to the Dragon Lady's lair. Paula had hooted when he'd used that description of Maria's office but had warned him not to use it too often.

'Too many little snitches around here,' she'd told him.

He tapped lightly on the door. "Good morning, Maria."

"Come in and sit down."

He glanced around as he entered. No Paula. *Uh oh, this can't be good…*

"The designs you left for me to see…" Maria pursed her lips and paused. "I don't like them."

"Really?" Justin arched an eyebrow. "You couldn't wait to get your hands on them the other day."

"I also don't like your tone."

"And I don't like the way you think you can insult my work," Justin snapped. "Look, I don't consider myself to be, say, world class, but I know I'm good and I know other people think so too. Tell me what it is you don't like about them and I'll see if I can fix them to your satisfaction."

"I don't like anything about them. They're not good enough for Esteban."

"Bullshit. Since when? I've been designing this cheap stuff for over a year. Your sales have gone up since you took me on. What? D'you think I'm an idiot and I don't know what you're doing? You want me to flounce outta here and leave my stuff behind. Well, that ain't gonna happen, Mrs. Esteban. I won't resign. You can fire me again if you like and pay my unemployment along with a severance settlement in lieu of my sales commissions. But I really have to wonder at your work ethics. Firing me, rehiring me and threatening to fire me again all in the space of a few days!"

"You are an arrogant little shit!"

"And you are—okay, I'm too nice a guy to tell you what I think of you." He got up from his seat opposite her. "Although the word 'shrew' comes to mind. Let me know what your decision is gonna be, but I'd talk it over with Paula, if I were you. She, at least, has some business savvy."

He left Maria seething at her desk and closed the door quietly behind him. He'd have loved to have slammed it, but that would be bringing himself down to her level. *What a bitch. No wonder her hubby can't stand her.*

Paula caught up with him in the hallway. "I heard what went on in there," she said. "Don't worry, she's not going to fire you."

"You know, Paula, at this point I really don't give a damn. She's become impossible to work for. I don't appreciate having my work insulted like that. The woman has no class."

Paula's cell rang at that moment and Justin was puzzled when she glanced at the screen and frowned but didn't take the call.

"Problem?"

"Oh, no…I'll deal with it later." She patted his arm. "Don't let her get to you, Justin. We all know your work is exemplary."

"Thanks. I think I'll take an early lunch break. Clear my head a bit. I'll see you later. Bye."

"Bye, Justin."

* * * *

Sam and Martin cruised around the streets near where Joey's body had been found. Sam wondered if Joey's death would stop some of the hustlers from coming out for a while, or did they have that 'it won't happen to me' syndrome so prevalent among street kids?

"There he is," Martin muttered. "You think he'll talk to us?"

"We can but try," Sam said, lowering his window as they drew up alongside the young hustler. "Hey, Rolando…"

He'd given the car an expectant look at first then, on seeing Sam, he scowled and started to walk away.

"Wait up, Rolando." Sam was out of the car and trailing behind him. "We want to talk to you about Joey Carter."

"He's dead." Rolando swung around to face Sam. "What's to talk about unless it's to tell me you found the fucker that killed him?"

"I'm sorry I can't tell you that, yet." Sam stared into Rolando's gray eyes. "We want to catch his killer. If there's anything you can tell us, please do. Do you know of anyone who might have had a grudge against him…enough to kill him?"

Rolando shook his head. "Could've been anybody. A pimp, a john, a *cop*." He met Sam's stare with a hostile look. "You guys all stick together, cover for one another. I seen you the other night, y'know, chasing that cop with the kid outta the park. He's been here before, and that punk kid and his punk friends. They tried to beat the shit outta some of us one night. Four of 'em, but we took the fuckers down and they ran like the fucking cowards they are. They set that kid up the other night. Some friends he has—"

"Wait, you're saying Detective Sanders' nephew and friends of his were up here messing with you guys?" Martin gripped Sam's arm. "Sanders has to be out of his freakin' mind."

"Was he trying to stop the attack?" Sam asked.

"No, that mofo was encouraging them till we had them on the run. Then he grabbed the kid you saw him with and drove off."

"Rolando…" Sam kept his voice low. "Why didn't you tell us about this the other night?"

"Because cops never believe us, 'specially if it's about another cop. All they do is harass us or try to proposition us for a free blowjob. You think we want this life, Detective? Maybe Joey's better off." He glared at Sam. "He tried to kill himself, you know, a few weeks ago."

"No, I didn't know. I'm sorry, Rolando."

"Yeah, well it's too late now for *sorry*. A bit like *thoughts and prayers* isn't it?" He walked away before Sam could say anything further, and Sam watched him go, feeling like shit.

"Damn," he muttered, and Martin echoed him.

"Fucking Sanders, man," he said. "We have to report this. Get the captain to question him."

Sam nodded and pulled out his cell. "He's on night duty. I'll tell him we have to see him soon as we get back to the precinct."

* * * *

Hoskins stared at them his expression one of anger mixed with disbelief.

"We might have found it harder to believe, Captain, if we hadn't seen him in the park with his nephew a couple of nights ago," Sam said while Hoskins slumped back in his chair and gazed into space.

"He's been on report a couple of times previous, but not for anything like this." Hoskins twiddled with the pen in his hand. "How involved d'you think he is?"

Martin shook his head. "Hard to say. It could be just harassing the kids, or…it could something more."

"Regardless, what he's up to with his nephew and buddies is illegal," Sam snapped. "The guy is a disgrace to the department and should be fired at the very least."

Hoskins nodded. "I'll have him brought in and put on suspension till we get all the facts. You think Mackie's in on this?"

"Rolando only mentioned Sanders as being at the scene of the attack, but Mackie did drive Sanders and the nephew from the park the other night," Sam said.

"And he did hear Kirby grip say he and his buds were fixing to beat up some hustlers and he didn't say a word," Martin added. "Didn't even flinch."

"Maybe he was too surprised to say anything," Sam suggested.

Hoskins arched an eyebrow. "Kirby grip?"

"The nephew's name is Kirby," Martin explained. "I added the 'grip' to piss the little bigot off."

"Oh." Hoskins' mouth quirked at the corner while he twiddled with his pen some more. "Well, I'll question Mackie separately. I'll have them brought in for questioning tomorrow morning. You two will not be present but you may be called in at some point. I don't want Sanders to know you're in on this…yet."

"Okay, Captain."

On the way out, Sam said, "We better get back to the park."

"You don't think Sanders is gonna show up again, do you?"

"No, even he couldn't be that dumb."

"Maybe he killed Joey Carter," Martin mused.

"The guy's a creep, but I don't think he's a murderer, Martin. He's just a homophobe using what power he thinks he has to impress his nephew. The kid goes along with it 'cause he can in turn impress his friends and they think they can't get in trouble 'cause Uncle Eliot is a cop."

Martin nodded as they climbed into their car. "I'm still gonna punch his lights out after they fire him. I just hope Mackie's not involved."

Chapter Eight

The park was quiet as they cruised the perimeter. Only a couple of boys, one tall and black, the other white and about a head shorter, stood smoking and shooting the breeze on one corner. They eyed the car with suspicion at first but then the shorter of the two approached after a minute or so had gone by.

"You guys lookin' for some action?" he asked.

"We're cops," Martin said.

"Shit!" The kid turned to run, but Sam got out of the car and yelled, "Wait. We won't book you. Just need to ask a couple of questions."

The taller of the two took off at a fast clip, but the one who'd propositioned them faced Sam and shrugged. "What kinda questions? How much for a bj?"

Sam took in the fair hair and the pug nose. "You Mikey?"

"Yeah." He gave Sam a teasing smile.

"Mikey, we've been looking for you."

"Oh yeah? So now you've found me. You're kinda hot. You don't look like you'd kill me."

Sam shook his head. "You guys take a lot of chances. After what happened to Joey, I thought you would be more careful."

"That's why I was with Clyde. We figured safety in numbers, ya know?"

"You were a friend of Joey Carter."

Mikey's face fell. "Yeah. Joey… Fuckin' shame, but he should've been more careful who he hung out with. 'Specially the big dude I seen him with sometimes."

"This big dude. You know who he is?"

"Think his name is Dwight. Him and his bro are dealers. They come sniffing around the park looking to sell some shit, get a free blowjob. They're big and rough, scary dudes. I blew one of them one night and never again. He almost broke my neck…then the mofo stiffed me. I told Joey to have nothing to do with them, but he seemed to like Dwight."

Sam glanced at Martin, who had got out of the car. "Describe him for us."

"I'd say he's way over six feet, taller even than you guys. He has red hair, the one called Dwight."

"You remember what this Dwight was wearing the night you saw him with Joey?"

"I think he was wearing like a bomber jacket, kinda tweedy lookin'. That's all I could see before they walked away together. We didn't notice Joey hadn't come back…we were kinda busy, ya know."

Martin sighed. "You guys…"

Sam understood Martin's despair, but he also understood the situation Mikey and others had found themselves in. "You have family, Mikey?" He knew the answer before Mikey shook his head.

"Naw, my dad threw me and my mom out. He'd found another woman and couldn't afford us, he said.

My mom died of a drug overdose about a year ago. I've been on my own since then 'cept for Clyde. We have a room together."

"Can't you guys get a decent job instead of putting your lives in danger out here?"

Mikey stared at Martin and laughed. "There's no jobs if you didn't graduate high school 'cept maybe McDonald's or Walmart. No thanks. This ain't the greatest, but at least I don't have to answer to some fat blowhard telling me what to do. Out here, I'm my own boss. Sometimes the john isn't bad lookin' and gives us an extra twenty."

Sam looked up as a figure approached. "You Clyde?"

"Yeah, whatcha doin' to my bro?"

"It's okay," Mikey said. He let Clyde put a protective arm around him. "For cops, they're not so bad."

"Listen, guys, would you come to the precinct with us and make a statement, look at some mugshots?" Sam knew what the answer would probably be, but he had to try. "I promise you won't get into any trouble."

Both boys tensed. "Naw, can't do that." Clyde was the first to refuse, shaking his head for emphasis. "No way, sorry." He started to back up dragging Mikey with him until they broke into a run, leaving Sam and Martin staring after them. Before long they'd disappeared into the street's dark shadows.

* * * *

"'Kay, Gus, see what wizardry you can drum up from this description." Sam handed Gus a note with what little they had on Joey's possible killer.

"Brothers, one maybe named Dwight. Six feet five or maybe more, red hair, drug related." Gus squinted up at him. "What the hell is this?"

"A long shot," Sam told him. "An eyewitness account of a possible killer. Make it work, O Gus, master of the database. If it can be done, you're the man to do it."

"Huh. Okay, no hovering. I'll bring you what I got *if* I find anything."

"We'll be by the coffee station, trying not to get poisoned," Martin told him, but Gus was already too involved to hear.

"He does love a challenge," Sam said as they strolled over to the coffee station.

They didn't have long to wait. "Hey, detectives." Gus waved them over to his computer on their return. "We might have hit paydirt with a couple of these. Take a looksee."

Sam studied the mugshots Gus had brought up on his screen. "Interesting. The one on the left did three years for burglary and pushing drugs, the one on the right five years for drugs and aggravated assault. But look at the faces. They're definitely brothers, maybe even twins, even though they have different last names."

"Yeah, Dwight Rothman and Darius Hellman," Martin said, his hand on Sam's shoulder as he leaned in closer to the screen. "Current status, Rothman has one year left of a three-year parole and Hellman just got out by the looks of things. He's on parole for the next five years."

"And they have the same address."

Martin grinned at him. "That's convenient. We only have one call to make."

* * * *

The address on Rugby Drive in West Hollywood was a ground floor apartment in a white stuccoed building surrounded by flaming red bougainvillea and yucca plants.

"Doesn't quite fit, does it?" Sam muttered as they got out of the car and walked up the short path to a wrought-iron gate. He pushed the gate open and approached the door to apartment 1C. His knock was answered by an elderly woman's voice quavering "Who is it?"

"LAPD detectives, ma'am. You have a minute?"

The door opened a fraction and the old lady peeked out. "Yes?"

"We're looking for a Dwight Rothman or a Darius Hellman. Do you know either of those men?"

She nodded. "What have they done now?"

"Uh, well, we really wanted to ask them a few questions," Sam said. "But sounds like you do know them."

"They're my grandsons, more's the pity."

Sam glanced at Martin. "Do you know where we might find them?"

"If you'd been here an hour ago, you'd have run right into them. But I don't know where they get to once they leave here."

"Would you mind if we took a look around? They have a room here?" Sam smiled at the old lady to put her at ease.

"I guess so. It'll be a mess. I haven't the energy to clean up after them anymore." She opened the door wider. "Come on in."

Sam stepped inside and nearly tripped over a large gray cat that spat at him. "Sorry," he mumbled. "Didn't see him there." He produced his ID. "I'm Detective Sam

Walker and this is my partner Detective Martin McCready."

"Pleased to meet you, I'm sure."

"So what do your grandsons do for a living, Mrs., uh…"

She rolled her eyes at Martin. "Mrs. Bassinger…and God alone knows what those two do when they leave this house. Something illegal I bet, but long as I don't know about it I don't really care. They pay the rent on time so that's good."

"Can we take a look at their room?" Sam asked.

"Shouldn't you have a warrant?"

"We could get one, but seeing as we're here…with your permission?"

"Right. Okay then go ahead, but like I said it's a mess."

Sam whistled softly as he threw open the door to the brothers' room. Two beds almost filled the space and there were clothes, shoes and magazines piled on top of them and over the floor.

"The only thing you won't find in there is junk food containers." Mrs. Bassinger peered into the room and shook her head. "I don't allow them to eat in there. They have to use the kitchen. Don't want no roaches."

"Good idea," Martin told her, trying to squeeze in beside Sam. "How in hell do two big bruisers like them manage in here?" he whispered practically in Sam's ear.

Sam chuckled. "Dunno, but it's the perfect cover for criminal activity. Tiny apartment, little old lady who answers the door." He inched his way past the beds to a table covered in papers. "Look at this." He held up a notepad. "Names and addresses of properties in Beverly Hills and Hollywood Hills."

"Are your grandsons in real estate?" Sam asked, grinning at Martin.

"No, God knows what they're in," Mrs. Bassinger replied. "Probably clients." She frowned, seeing Sam taking snapshots of the pages. "Should you be doing that without a warrant?"

"What kind of clients?" Martin asked.

"Oh, I have no idea." Mrs. Bassinger fluttered her hands. "You boys are making me nervous. Maybe you should go."

"Okay, ma'am, and we thank you for your time." Sam was about to head for the door when he caught sight of a tiny sparkle on the floor. He bent as if he was tying his shoelace and palmed the gem. When he straightened up he smiled at the old lady. "Thank you again, ma'am. No need to tell your grandsons we were here if it'll cause you trouble."

"I think you're right. They might not be too pleased," she said, closing the door behind them.

"And that's an understatement," Martin muttered. "What did you pick up?"

Sam handed him the small jewel. "An earring. Seen it before?"

Martin stared at it then at Sam, his eyes widening. "Fuck me. Looks like a match for the one Joey Carter was wearing."

"I'd bet dollars to donuts that it's the same," Sam said. "It might have got tangled in whatever either Darius or Dwight had on."

"A tweed bomber, according to Mikey. Yeah, it could have got caught in that and never be noticed. Just fallen off when he threw the jacket down. One look at that room and you know they never hang anything up."

"Okay, so we got our probable killer."

"Right. Only thing is we can't use the list or the earring as evidence, seeing as how we had no warrant."

"We had Mrs. Bassinger's permission. We're good."

* * * *

When they got back to the precinct, Sam took a moment to call Justin. "How's it going, beautiful?" He kept his voice low as there were still a few officers and detectives wandering around or on their computers.

"Hey, Sam, so good to hear your voice."

"You sound down. That boss of yours still giving you problems?"

"'Fraid so, but I don't want to bore you with that, not when I only get a few minutes of your time."

"I'm sorry 'bout that. Martin and me will be winding this up in a few. I know it's late, but I could drop by if you like?"

"Like? I would *love* that, Sam."

"Good," Sam said, pleased as punch at Justin's enthusiasm. Once again he was getting hard just talking to Justin—or was it the anticipation of what they could share? Either way, he wouldn't be getting out from behind his desk until he absolutely had to.

After he finished the call with Justin he and Martin drew up their statements about what they had uncovered during their shift…the information from Mikey regarding the possible connection between Joey Carter and the Rothman/Hellman brothers. They included their suspicions that one or both of the brothers might also be responsible for Joey Carter's murder.

Hoskins had left them emails reminding them of Sanders being questioned in the morning at eleven a.m. and to be there to answer any further questions the interrogating agent might have.

"So who're you having all these little tête-à-têtes with on the phone, my man?" Martin asked as they left the precinct. "Don't think I haven't noticed those whispered conversations and that goofy smile on your face. 'Fess up now, boy. Who is it you're seeing?"

Sam groaned. "You're gonna tell Liz if I tell you and next time I see her she'll want *details*."

"Never mind her. *I* want details!" He grinned at Sam and squeezed his shoulder. "So there is someone, huh?"

"Real early in the game to say we're *seeing* each other, but yeah, there is a guy." *Oh, boy, is there a guy!*

"Fantastic. And just when were you going to share this news with your best partner ever?"

"When it got a little more, you know, solid."

"Solid? What is it now, like jello?"

Sam chuckled. "No definitely not like jello…it's just too soon to talk about it. You're the first to know, if that makes you feel better about it."

"Hmm, that's something, I guess. Well, Liz will be delighted to know it's finally happened."

"*Martin.* Let me be the one to tell her."

"Well, you better figure on doin' it tonight, 'cause soon as I walk in the door she'll know I have something to tell her. She can read me like a book. I have no defenses against her nosiness."

"Not tonight. Next time we're together."

"Okay, partner mine. I'll see you tomorra. Should be interesting."

"At the very least. G'night, Martin."

"'Night, Sam."

Chapter Nine

Sam made good time over to Justin's place. Seeing Justin, holding him, kissing him would be the perfect antidote to the end of a shitty day. Those kids out there setting themselves up to be taken advantage of, often lost and alone…when he dwelt on it too long it near broke his heart. *It could've been me…thank God for Kenny and his family, or I might have been the one out there all those years ago trolling the streets along with all the other lost boys.*

Okay, he couldn't meet Justin with an air of depression hanging over him. Justin had sounded as if he needed some cheering up, too. He put a bright smile on his face as the door was swung open.

"Hi," was all he managed before Justin was in his arms and their mouths were meshed in a kiss that left him in no doubt that Justin was pleased to see him. More than pleased if the hardness behind the skimpy shorts he was wearing was any indication. Sam let himself be pulled into the living room. His T-shirt was tugged up over his head and thrown to one side. Then Justin's lips were on Sam's neck, his throat, his chest, his nipples and he could do nothing but give himself up to the visceral sensations that holding this lithe and supple body pressed to his own brought him.

"Justin," he breathed into his lover's mouth.

"Yeah, I know." Justin's whisper tickled Sam's lips "I'm so glad you're here." He leaned back a little. "I waited, thinking you might want to shower."

"That'd be good."

"Together."

"That'd be even better."

Sam stepped out of his boots, jeans and briefs while he and Justin hurried to the bathroom, despite the fact that they had their arms around each other. *Amazing what you can do when you're good and eager…*

Once they were inside the stall and the hot water cascaded over them, their bodies came together in a bone-crushing embrace that had Justin writhing against Sam and his tongue searching out every corner of Sam's mouth. When they came up for air, Sam reached for the bodywash and upended the bottle over Justin's chest then rubbed it all over his torso down to his cock and balls. He skimmed his hands down the length of Justin's spine then cupped his sweet ass, pulling him in tight, fingering the cleft. Justin whimpered and pressed down into the pressure of Sam's finger, drawing him in. Their bodies slid together, their erections ground against each other and the urge to fuck Justin overwhelmed Sam.

"Yes, please," Justin whispered.

"What, you're reading minds now?"

"Only dirty ones," Justin said, chuckling.

Sam growled and shoved his finger farther up Justin's ass, curling it over his prostate and wrenching a long moan from him.

"Jesus, Sam…I'll come too soon if you keep doing that. I want that big cock of yours up there."

"Dirty boy."

"*Your* dirty boy, Sam."

"That's right." He tightened his arms around Justin and pressed his lips to Justin's mouth, tangling their tongues together, kissing him long and hard, reveling in the feel of Justin's roving hands as he caressed and stroked Sam's body.

"Come on," he said, breathing heavily. "Let's get you dried and ready for me." If anyone had told him he'd be rampantly horny and have the wherewithal to perform close to ten times in three days, he'd have laughed in their face. Sometimes he still couldn't believe it, but standing there running a towel over Justin's limber body, the evidence of his readiness pressed against Justin's thigh, what was there to not believe? *What's that old saying, 'All it takes is the right one' or something like that?*

"There you go thinking again. I can practically hear the gears turning."

Sam laughed and slapped Justin's butt. "I hear you thinking, too, you know."

"Yeah, well, now is the time for *action*, not thinking." He jumped into Sam's arms and wound his legs around Sam's narrow waist. "We can think and talk after you've fucked me."

"Wanna rim you first," Sam murmured, laying Justin on the bed face-down. "You like it?"

"Oh, yeah, specially the way you do it." He turned his head to look at Sam. "You sure you haven't had a whole heap of sex before me?"

Sam chuckled. "I'm sure. You're just lucky that I love spending time *exploring* you. I'm learning as I go."

Justin laughed. "So, go, Sam, go."

Sam dived in and Joey squirmed under him as Sam scoured the cleft between Joey's buttocks with his tongue. *Sweet…* He palmed each butt cheek, parting them to gain better access to the sensitive nerve endings surrounding Justin's hole. Justin groaned and his hips bucked when Sam pushed in, using the tip of his tongue to probe and tease.

"Sam, Sam," Justin moaned, raising his ass to encourage Sam to go deeper. Sam held Justin's hips steady and he plunged his tongue in and out of Justin's ass. Justin's body tensed and he gripped the sheet under him while he keened out a low cry of ecstasy. Sam reached for the lube and condom on top of the nightstand. Justin jumped when a cool, lubed finger replaced Sam's warm tongue, but he was smiling when Sam turned him onto his back. He raised his legs and hooked his ankles over Sam's shoulders, watching avidly while Sam sheathed and lubed himself. Sam leaned forward, placed a hand on either side of Justin's head and pushed forward. He loved to see the look in Justin's eyes as he penetrated him. That blink of surprise, the slow widening of his pupils when pleasure hit and the gleam that filled them as Sam slid all the way in.

"Saaam," he breathed shakily then wound his arms around Sam's neck and joined their lips together in a kiss that was tender at first but when their bodies moved to an erotic rhythm, that kiss became demanding, bruising, in a clash of lips, teeth and tongues. Lust-driven, Sam rammed his cock deep into Justin's heat, every thrust bringing him closer to the point of no return. Justin clung to him, his arms and legs wrapped tight around Sam's torso. Sam eased one hand between their bodies to grip Justin's erection, which was slick with pre-cum.

"Come with me," he whispered in Justin's ear.

As the rhythm of their lovemaking increased its pace, Justin arched his body into Sam's, clinging to him like a limpet, riding the bucking motion of Sam's thrusts and claiming each one with an upward push of his hips. Sam pumped Justin's cock, willing him to climax as the urge to come overwhelmed him. Justin came first, calling out Sam's name when his hot seed jetted from him and coated his chest. Sam was ready now, unable to fight the spreading tingling that coasted down his spine and wrapped around his balls. He plunged again and again inside Justin until with a wild cry he came, his orgasm wrenched from with mind-blowing force

Panting, he gazed down at Justin's face, which seemed to him to be even more beautiful, his cheeks flushed from his climax, his lips swollen from the myriad kisses they had shared. He dipped his head to reach the glistening pools of cum on Justin's chest and trailed his tongue through them then placed a kiss on Justin's lips. Justin opened to him and their tongues tangled and Justin tightened his arms around Sam as they shared Justin's salty essence.

"So good," Sam murmured on Justin's lips.

"Yes, you are," Justin replied.

Afterward they lay side by side, arms around each other, Sam's lips pressed to Justin's temple, and once again Sam marveled at just how amazingly perfect the sex was he had with him. *Best sex ever…*

"Yes, it is," Justin murmured. "The very best."

"Did you just read my mind…again?"

"No, you said, the best sex ever and I agreed. What, you didn't mean to say it?"

Sam chuckled. "I thought I was thinking it. Must have slipped out."

"You're funny." Justin kissed Sam's chest. "Funny and fantastic."

"But I meant it, Justin. Truly, every time with you, it's the best I've ever known."

Justin raised his head and smiled at Sam. "I like that." He parted his lips, an invitation that Sam was not about to refuse. Their kiss was sweet, tender, yet with an underlying layer of passion that made Sam feel things he'd never felt before Justin. Despite the vagaries and stress of working in law enforcement for the last few days, he'd also experienced a sense of euphoria, and he couldn't remember having that feeling…ever.

Justin climbed on top of him and, before he could say 'sex', they were doing it again.

* * * *

"So tell me what happened that made you unhappy today." Sam thought after that second round they should take it easy and talk for a while.

Justin sighed. "Not unhappy…frustrated. The woman I work for is kinda nuts. Last week she fired me then called and said she'd made a mistake and would I come back. I have nothing else so I said yes, and this morning soon as I got there, she starts telling me my designs are no good…the same ones she wanted me to leave behind. We got into a bit of a spat. Paula, her secretary, told me she's having marital problems, but why take that out on me? Honestly, Sam, I have to look for something else. She gets me mad, and I don't like working in that kind of atmosphere."

Sam stroked Justin's hair and kissed his forehead. "Yeah, it's shitty when you don't enjoy going to work."

"I love what I do, Sam, but not where I'm doing it." He pushed his head into Sam's stroking hand. "I just have to keep on putting my résumé out there and pray that something good comes along. I mean…" He smiled into Sam's eyes. "It could happen. I prayed for someone like you, and here you are."

"You and that silver tongue," Sam said smiling.

"Every word is true." He kissed Sam. "But you…you have a whole lot more going on than I do."

Sam nodded. "Martin and I are investigating a case of a murdered kid who got mixed up with the wrong people."

"Oh, God, that's terrible."

"Yeah, he was only eighteen, homeless, hustling to get by…"

Justin sighed. "God, and here am I thinking my life is hard, and what do I have to complain about really? A whiny bitch of a boss is all, but there are kids out there whose lives are in actual danger and they have no one to turn to. At least I know if I'm ever in trouble I have my family…and now you, of course." He laid a gentle kiss on Sam's lips.

Sam tightened his arms around Justin. He couldn't imagine what kind of trouble Justin could get himself into, but he was right—he'd be there for him, no matter what.

* * * *

Sam met Martin at the precinct at ten-thirty in the morning. They had spoken on the phone to arrange their day. First, be available for the time when Sanders would face Captain Hoskins and an investigator from headquarters who would have been apprised of the charges to be brought against Sanders. That guy was already in Hoskins' office, presumably going over the necessary paperwork. Once whatever would happen to Sanders was out of the way, they were going back to Mrs. Bassinger's apartment for, no doubt, a confrontation with her grandsons. Sam wondered if she'd mentioned their visit to the guys, and somehow he doubted that she had. She hadn't come across as super happy to have them living with her and certainly didn't approve of their life choices. Still…blood often proved to be thicker than water.

He and Martin traded looks when Sanders marched into the office area, his face like thunder, and went straight to Hoskins' door, rapping on it sharply. He disappeared inside and it wasn't long before Sam, Martin and everybody else in the office heard an angry voice raised in protest. The door was flung open and Sanders stormed out followed by Hoskins and the investigating officer.

"You fuckers did this, didn't you?" he screamed, pointing a finger at Sam and Martin.

"Did what, exactly?" Sam kept his expression neutral as he looked at the furious detective.

"You went to the captain with some cockamamie shit story about me allowing my nephew and his friends to beat on some punks." Sanders appeared about to implode. "Fuckin' lies and you know it."

"We talked to an eyewitness, Sanders," Martin said. "He told us about the attack and also told us that the night we saw you and your nephew in the park, Kirby had been set up by his friends, if you could call them that. They were supposed to meet him there and beat up on the kids in the park."

"Okay." Hoskins stepped forward. "Back in my office, Sanders. You two also. Let's go."

They trooped into Hoskins' office, which wasn't exactly designed to accommodate five big men. Hoskins and the investigating officer, who introduced himself as Harold Wentworth, sat behind the desk, Sanders pushed the chair he'd been sitting on up against the wall and sat, while Sam and Martin ranged themselves against the far wall. The atmosphere, thick with tension, could have been cut with a knife.

"Ask Mackie," Sanders exclaimed. "He was with me the night I picked Kirby up at the park."

"We intend talking to Detective Mackie later today," Wentworth said. "First I want to hear from the detectives about this eyewitness to the alleged attack." He looked to Sam and Martin. "What is this person's name?"

"Rolando Lopez."

"Sounds like an illegal," Sanders spat.

Sam rolled his eyes. "Sanders, surely even you don't think that a Hispanic name means a person is an illegal."

"That's right, Detective." Hoskins glared at him. "This is no time to be displaying that kind of prejudice."

This guy is going to bury himself, Sam thought. "Rolando Lopez is a hustler, but he is an American citizen. He told us that your nephew and a bunch of kids attacked some of the hustlers, friends of Joey Carter, the kid that was found murdered yesterday morning."

Sanders face suddenly lost a lot of color. "I—I don't know anything about that," he spluttered.

"But do you know about the attack Detectives Walker and McCready reported to Captain Hoskins?" Wentworth asked. "Were your nephew and his friends involved in that? Think before you answer, Detective. There is an eyewitness to the attack."

"Several, if we can round them up," Martin said. "Some of Rolando's buddies busted the fight up, and he fingered you, Sanders, being there and the fact you drove your nephew from the scene."

"No way! No fucking way!" Sanders jumped to his feet, his face once again beet-red. "You're lying, the both of you. You're just trying to protect those hustlers who should all be in jail. Filthy little fags, all of them." He regarded Sam balefully. "Of course, *you* would want to protect them, being a fag yourself."

Beside Sam, Martin tensed and Sam put a hand on his partner's arm to restrain him. Much as he wanted to punch Sanders on the nose, this wasn't the place to do it.

"*Detective Sanders,*" Hoskins snapped. "That's enough of that kind of talk. You know it's against departmental rules—"

"And not only that," Wentworth interjected. "Disrespectful of a fellow officer. You will apologize right now to Detective Walker."

"Not on your life." Sanders sat down heavily on the chair behind him and scowled at everyone in the room.

Hoskins sighed. "Detective Sanders, I am putting you on suspension while an investigation is carried out as to your alleged illicit behavior and flagrant disobedience of departmental rules. You will hand over your badge and your gun immediately, and you will leave the precinct until further notice. Do it willingly or I will have you escorted out."

"There will be a formal inquiry, Detective," Wentworth said. "I would advise you to have legal counsel with you. It appears to me that you need guidance in how to behave under such conditions."

Sanders glared at him, opened his mouth then snapped it shut as if he'd thought better of what he'd been about to say. He stood and, without a word, handed over his badge and his gun then, with a final venomous look at Sam, strode out of the office.

"That went well," Martin muttered.

Hoskins sat back in his chair with a disgusted snort. "So, give me some good news."

Sam said, "It's possible we have found Joey Carter's killer."

"Oh yeah? Let's hope you're right. Keep me informed. I have to write a report on the case and have it upstairs no later than tomorrow afternoon."

"Will do, Captain," Martin said. "Anything else for us?"

"No, that'll be it for now."

"Okay." Sam nodded at Wentworth. "Nice meeting you, sir."

"A pity about the circumstances, but nice meeting both you and Detective McCready." Wentworth stood to shake their hands. "Good luck with the case you're working on."

Chapter Ten

"So..." Sam clapped Martin on the back as they walked back to their desks. "How d'you want to do this?"

"I say I'll hold him down and you stomp the shit outta him."

Sam laughed. "Not Sanders, my friend, the ginger boys."

"Same thing, they're all scum, but..." He grinned at Sam. "They have to have their day in court so I'll be good and play by the rules...this time."

"Of course you will. That's what we do." Sam picked up the keys to their car and made for the exit. "We'll talk about strategy on the way."

Martin snorted. "Yeah, strategy, right."

On the way over Sam asked how Liz and the kids were doing and Martin said 'fine' and they were expecting him to stop by. "At least Sara and Abe are, looking for some gifts from Unca Sam of course. And Liz will want to hear all about the guy you're waiting to get solid with."

Martin cackled. "*Solid* with! Oh boy, I crack myself up sometimes."

Sam scowled at him. "You are so not funny."

"Yes, I am, man. *Solid with.*"

Sam tried hard not to chuckle, but in the end he had to give in, more because he appreciated Martin's easygoing attitude than anything else. They were still laughing when Sam pulled up outside Grandma Bassinger's apartment building.

"So, here goes nothing," he muttered as they walked the few steps to the front door.

"Who is it?" Sam recognized the elderly woman's voice answering his knock.

"Sam Walker, ma'am."

"Who?" She opened the door anyway and Sam flinched when he saw the bruising on her left cheek.

Those sons of bitches. He flashed his badge and put his finger to his lips at the same time. "Are they here?"

"Dead to the world. They came home drunk as skunks last night and wrecked my living room." She pulled the door open wider. "Look what they did. And I don't have the strength to lift any of that stuff."

Sam and Martin stepped inside and Martin swore under his breath. Wrecked was the right word. Every piece of furniture had been upended, broken glass scattered everywhere and Mrs. Bassinger in tears.

"Why'd they do this?" Sam asked, keeping his voice low.

"Some business deal gone sour. I managed to get that much before they went berserk. Why the hell they couldn't have busted up a bar instead, I don't know."

"Okay, ma'am. I want you to step outside for a few minutes. Can you go visit a neighbor or something?"

She nodded. "Mrs. Castaña will be home."

"We'll come get you when it's all clear, okay?"

She nodded again and slipped out through the front door. Sam shook his head, watching her go. "Those bastards. Let's get 'em, Martin."

They used no stealth, just kicked the bedroom door open, guns drawn.

"What the fuck?" Two surly faces greeted them, bleary-eyed and bloated. The room stank like a brewery.

"Up!" Martin commanded. "Hands where we can see them. Jesus!" Two naked hulks sprouting morning wood was obviously too much for Martin's eyes. "Put something on, for Chrissakes."

Sam's first instinct to laugh died as he caught a furtive move from the taller brother. Somehow he'd got a gun in his hand and it was pointed straight at Martin's chest. The roar of the gunshot in the that small room was deafening. Martin went down, but so did the gunman when Sam shot him. The other brother screamed and lunged for Sam, who collapsed under the sheer weight of the man. Sam gagged at the combined stench of the suspect's rank body odor and boozy breath. He rammed his gun into the side of the giant's head and dazed him enough that he was able to wriggle out from under the naked body.

He thanked the gods that they'd had the foresight to have a black and white follow them to the address. Two police officers barreled into the room.

"Cuff that one," Sam barked then called 9-1-1. He reeled off the need for an ambulance, giving the responder the address and details of the emergency. He knelt by Martin's side, feeling for a pulse.

Oh, dear God, please don't be dead, Martin, please… There was a pulse, weak, but it was there. But there was so much blood.

Martin.

"This one's dead," one of the officers said, indicating the brother Sam had shot.

"Call it in." Sam sat on the floor by his partner's side, holding his hand while he waited for the paramedics to arrive.

* * * *

He called Liz from the hospital and she was there within a half hour. His words of comfort seemed hollow to his own ears, but she clung to him as she sobbed, oblivious to the other detectives and police officers who had gathered in the waiting room, hoping for good news but fearing the worst. He couldn't even utter the platitudes so many thought necessary at moments like this. *He's a fighter, he'll pull through, don't worry, it'll be okay, just you wait and see.*

They sat side by side, Liz's head on his shoulder, not saying very much at all while Sam went over and over in his head how this could all have been avoided. Had they been too cavalier, too sure that they could take down two drunks without giving enough thought to how it could so easily go wrong?

Truth be told, Sam hadn't expected them to be crazy enough to try and shoot their way out. Nothing on their record had indicated armed violence, but criminals could often be reckless, not wanting to face more years behind bars. *Guess they reacted like the cornered rats they are. Kill the cops and get the fuck out.*

"The kids being looked after?" he asked, thinking what a dumb question it was.

"They're with my sister." Liz leaned her head on his shoulder. "It's his thirty-fifth birthday next month," she murmured. "We were going to have a party. Have you and some of the other guys over. His mom and dad are flying from Atlanta...oh God, I have to tell them it's off...it's..."

He put his arm around her. "We'll still have the party, Liz. I know Martin's gonna be okay. I told him he had to be for your sake and the kids...and me..." They held each other as they cried together. Sam didn't give a damn that all the other men and women in the waiting room could see him sobbing his heart out. It was Martin after all, his partner, his best friend. Until Justin, his only friend, really.

He jumped when a loud voice called out, "Mrs. McCready!" Liz sprang to her feet and grabbed Sam's hand, forcing him to stand also.

"If you'd like to come with me, Mrs. McCready." The doctor, tall and reed-thin, gave her a benign smile.

"Sam has to come too," Liz said. "He's Martin's partner and I need him right now."

The doctor nodded and led the way through a door into a long hall, Sam and Liz following in his wake. They entered a room in ICU and Sam felt physically sick at the sight of his partner hooked up to just about every available machine he could imagine. He put an arm around a trembling Liz while the doctor intoned Martin's diagnosis.

"But the good news, Mrs. McCready, is that your husband will survive. The bullet passed close to his heart but missed the important arteries. Most of the damage is in tissue and bone which of course will take a considerable amount of time to heal. His recovery will be slow and painful, but he will recover."

Liz all but collapsed against Sam. "Oh, thank God, thank God," she murmured over and over. Sam led her over to the chair by Martin's bed. "Thanks for the good news, Doc," he said, staring at Martin and finding it hard to believe that the man lying there so still and vulnerable was the same one who just a few hours ago had been a formidable presence in their confrontation with Mrs. Bassinger's grandsons.

"Told you he'd be all right," he whispered close to Liz's ear. "He's way too ornery to let a bullet stop him."

Liz nodded and laid her hand over Martin's, squeezing gently. "It's funny. The times I've worried about him getting hurt…and you too, Sam. I knew it was probably on the cards and I wondered how I'd deal with it…"

"And now you're gonna have to deal with him getting better. And you know as well as I do he is gonna be one grouchy bear when he comes to." Sam figured some levity was due and he was relieved when Liz smiled. "You be all right if I go tell the guys how he's doing?"

Liz nodded. "And I know you have things to take care of, so don't worry 'bout me. I'll be fine right here now I know he's gonna be okay."

He dropped a kiss on her cheek. "I'll stop by later and check up on you both."

He went back to the waiting room and was immediately surrounded by officers and detectives wanting to know how Martin was doing. Once he'd given out the news, Hoskins steered him to the exit.

"We need to question Dwight Rothman ASAP and get him booked as an accessory to shooting McCready. I've been over the scene. The old lady's in shock, of course, but she's going to stay with the neighbor until forensics are through and I can get the place cleaned up some. I've got officers checking out that list of addresses you found and sent me copies of. An officer has already reported in that the owners of two of the houses he visited had attempted break-ins. One of them has a dog that took a bite outta some guy climbing the perimeter wall."

"Darius Hellman had a bandaged arm," Sam told him.

"Oh yeah? We'll have the coroner check for teeth marks. But here's the deal. We found a shit-ton of cocaine in a suitcase under one of the beds. Street value around two hundred grand."

Sam whistled through is teeth. "So we got Rothman on drug dealing plus being an accessory. Once we get him for Joey Carter's murder, he's never comin' out!"

* * * *

Dwight Rothman cast Sam and Hoskins surly looks when they entered the interrogation room. A nervous sandy-haired young man sat alongside him.

"I'm Alex Hardy, Mr. Rothman's attorney."

Poor you, Sam thought. They'd let Rothman dress in a T-shirt and shorts, but he still stank of booze and Hardy was not happy about it, from the look on his face. Someone had stuck a Band-Aid on the left side of Rothman's forehead where Sam's gun had collided with his skull, but there were two more bruises on his right cheek.

"Right, let's get to it," Hoskins said. He passed the notebook the police officers had taken from Rothman's room across the table in front of Rothman. "In addition to charging you with being an accessory in the attempted murder of Detective McCready, what can you tell us about these addresses?"

Rothman barely looked at it. "They're people's houses, I guess."

"And why were they on a list in your room?"

Rothman shrugged. "Something my bro was doing, maybe."

"And what might that be?"

"I dunno. His business."

"And yours," Hoskins snapped. "Two of the houses on the list had recently been broken into. The owner's dog took a bite outta the burglar's arm. Your bro has a bandage on his arm. What is the coroner gonna find under that bandage?"

"Shit if I know," Rothman snarled. "What am I, my brother's keeper?"

Hardy gaped at him then threw Sam and the captain a worried look.

"Okay. Tell me, Dwight, how'd you come by those bruises on the right side of your face?"

"I don't remember."

Sam smiled wryly. "Let me help you remember. Do you own a bomber jacket made of a kind of tweed material?"

"What of it?"

"Do you, or do you not, own a jacket like the one I just described?"

"Maybe."

"And did you know a young man named Joey Carter?"

"Detective…" Hardy butted in. "What has this to do with the charges against my client?"

"I'm adding a new charge," Sam said, fixing his eyes on Dwight Rothman. "One of murder."

"What?" Hardy's eyes bugged out of his head while Rothman stood so suddenly the chair he'd been sitting on careened against the wall.

Hoskins stood also. "Sit down, Rothman."

Calmly, Sam said, "Dwight Rothman, I'm arresting you for the murder of Joey Carter." He read the fuming man his rights while the police officer in the room forced him back into his chair and cuffed him.

"Now, where were you three nights ago around midnight?" Sam asked.

"Nowhere near Joey fucking Carter!"

"I have an eyewitness who saw you talking with Joey before the two of you walked off toward Santa Monica Boulevard. Some hours later, Joey was found strangled by someone so strong, his larynx was crushed. You fit the bill nicely enough, Dwight. Under Joey's fingernails were found threads and fibers of a rougher than usual material. Tweed fits that description nicely as well."

"The jacket's not mine. It belonged to Darius," Dwight snarled.

"Bring the jacket in," Hoskins told the police officer. "We'll have you try it on for size." He glanced at Hardy. "No objections, I trust?"

"None." Hardy looked like he was wishing this would be over soon.

The officer returned with the jacket and handed it to Rothman. "Put it on," Hoskins said.

Sam watched with wry amusement as Rothman pretended to have a problem struggling into the jacket. "If anything, it should be too big for you if it's your bro's," he remarked. "Don't try an O.J. on us, Dwight—just put the jacket on."

Rothman scowled but finally finished putting it on. It was a perfect fit. "So, what does this prove? Only that the jacket's mine. It doesn't mean I killed the kid."

"If the fibers under Joey's fingernails are a match for your jacket, it sure as hell puts you at the scene, Dwight."

Sam reached into his pocket. "But I have one more tiny piece to show you." He put Joey's earring on the table.

"What the fuck is that?"

"It's an earring, Dwight," Sam said, quietly. "Joey's earring. I found it on your bedroom floor. If you look carefully, there's a thread caught between the stone and the setting. I think it might match what the coroner found under Joey's fingernails. It must have caught on your jacket sleeve or maybe the lapel when you were manhandling Joey. What, you didn't want to pay for his services, you thought you'd get some for free? The coroner said Joey must've put up quite a fight against his assailant. I know I hit you, but what about the bruises on your right cheek? How'd you get those, Dwight? Did Joey manage to get in a couple of punches when you had him by the throat?"

Rothman swung around to face his attorney, who slid back on his seat, almost falling off the chair. "You gotta get me a deal. I have a grandmother I need to look after. She—"

Sam's loud laughter had Rothman half-rising out of his seat until the officer clamped his hands on the criminal's shoulders and sat him back down again.

"Of all the things you could've said, Dwight, that really is the dumbest. It's my bet that Mrs. Bassinger will not miss you for a second. No deal to help out your very nice grandmother."

"Right." Hoskins stood, indicating the interview was over. "You'll have a hearing tomorrow and we'll be asking that you be held without bail until trial."

"Wait, what about a deal?" Rothman was shaking and for a moment Sam thought he might just burst into tears.

"No deal, unless your attorney can work one out for you," Hoskins said. "However, I doubt that. Take the jacket off—we need to give it to forensics—then go with Officer Briggs. You'll be our guest for a while, Mr. Rothman."

Hardy, looking grim, nodded at them then followed Rothman out of the door.

"Must be his first case," Sam remarked.

"And how'd you like that shit about Rothman having to care for his grandmother?" Hoskins laughed nastily. "Like you said, the lady is better off without them."

Sam nodded but he couldn't ignore the irony behind the tragedy of Joey's murder. He'd just chosen the wrong guy to spend time with.

Chapter Eleven

"Visiting hours in the ICU are over at nine p.m., Detective Walker," the nurse in charge told him after she'd checked his badge.

"Is Mrs. McCready still here?"

"Yes, she'll be staying overnight."

"Could you ask if she'd come out and speak to me for a few minutes? I'd use my cell, but I don't want to make any unnecessary noise."

"Good of you. I'll go see if she's awake."

A few minutes later, Liz came through the doors and he got up to hug her. Then they sat together. "How is he?" Sam asked.

"Pretty much the same." She sighed. "Stable, thank God. Martha brought the kids over early this evening and she's keeping them till I can get home."

"Were they upset?"

"Sara cried, but Abe said Daddy looked like a spaceman with the mask on."

"Maybe I can go see them tomorrow. Do you need anything? Fresh clothes…stuff?"

Liz chuckled. "Martha's taking care of me and the kids. Don't you worry—you have enough going on without worrying 'bout me and the kids. Martin's gonna be fine, so you look after yourself, you hear?"

Sam nodded. "If Martin wakes up before I see him, tell him Dwight Rothman has been charged with Joey's murder. Might make him feel better."

* * * *

The following morning, he went in early to enter his report on his computer and send a copy to Hoskins. Mackie, Sanders' partner, entered and walked to his desk. The man hesitated for a couple of seconds then came over to Sam's desk.

"Sorry to hear about McCready," Mackie said, fidgeting slightly. "How's he doing?"

"He'll live. It's gonna take some time before he's back on duty, but at least he survived."

Mackie nodded. "You hear about Sanders?"

"Nope."

"He's on desk duty up in admin till they set a date for an inquiry."

"I'm glad you weren't mixed up in that shit with him. Didn't sound like you."

"Thanks. Yeah, that night you and McCready confronted us, he'd asked me to drive him over to the park. Kirby's mother was kinda frantic about the late hour."

"I wonder how frantic she's gonna be when she finds out her brother encouraged her son to go out gay-bashing?"

Mackie shook his head. "Just between you and me, I was never comfortable having Sanders as a partner. I envied you and McCready, Jones and Harrison and some of the other guys. You all seem to get along good, you know? Sanders is too much the right-winger. Some of the things he says about minorities…"

"I can imagine—and let's face it, he's not alone."

"Still, I really didn't want to hear it on a daily basis. Anyway, tell McCready I said hi when you go see him next."

"Will do."

He called Liz after Mackie went back to his desk. She sounded tired. "How's he doing?"

"He had a bad night," she told him, "but they've got him on some heavy drugs, so he's asleep right now."

"You wanna go home, get some rest? I can come by and sit with him. Looks like my day is pretty clear so far."

"You're so sweet, Sam, thanks, but I'm staying. You can come visit, of course."

"I'll come by after lunch. Maybe you could take a nap then or something."

After they hung up, Sam looked in on Hoskins to get the latest on Dwight Rothman and was gratified to know that the judge had set bail at a million dollars. No way would Rothman be good for that amount. He was going to stay in jail until his trial.

"At least Joey Carter's friends out there will know we didn't just sit on our thumbs and do nothing about his murder," Hoskins said. "They might feel easier about talking to us in the future."

"Maybe. But none of us are helped by the likes of Sanders encouraging his nephew to go beat them up just for kicks."

"You're right. Frankly, I don't know how he'll manage to talk himself out of the mess he created." He sighed. "On a brighter note, I talked with Liz McCready this morning and things are looking good. I'll get over to the hospital later today. You?"

"Yeah, Liz and I talked. I thought I'd relieve her this afternoon so she can catch a nap."

Hoskins gazed at him for a couple of moments. "You're a good guy, Sam. I know I probably don't say this enough, but I'm glad you and McCready are part of my team."

"Thanks, Captain, that means a lot."

Sam called Justin to see if he was available for lunch. This would be a first. The only time they'd been together was at night and for some hot sex. He wondered how Justin would react to seeing him in the cold light of day.

Jeez, low self-esteem, Sam? Maybe that therapist was right.

Before he chickened out and changed his mind, he punched in Justin's cell number. "Hey, Justin, wondered if you were available for lunch today?"

"You know just how to brighten my day."

It warmed Sam's heart to hear how eager Justin sounded. But he did catch the underlying tension in his voice.

"Things still rough?"

"You have no idea—but who cares? I'm going to have lunch with my favorite detective!"

Sam laughed. "Okay. Twelve sound good?"

"Excellent. How about Marino's? It's close enough for us both to walk there."

"Good choice. See you there."

"Can't wait."

Sam was smiling when he hung up. The guy made him feel warm all over from just the sound of his voice and the memory of his hot kisses. *Happy days are definitely here at last.*

* * * *

Marino's Downtown was a popular restaurant with a line outside already when Sam got there. He was really glad to see Justin waving at him from a table for two in the back.

"Wow, you must've gotten here early," he said, squeezing Justin's hand as he sat opposite him.

"I know the lady upfront. I designed a couple of dresses for her daughter and she was very complimentary. She saw me get in line and told me to follow her, so I did." He smiled at Sam. "You look great."

"You too. I like the colors on the shirt you have on."

"Thanks. One of my designs. I'm glad you like it."

"I also want to kiss you, but probably not a good idea right now."

Justin chuckled. "We could pretend to be French. I love the way they say hello with kisses."

"Mmm." Sam gazed at Justin. He could lose himself in those green eyes. "You know…" He pulled himself together. "This is a first for us, meeting in the daytime, having lunch. I can't remember the last time I did anything so civilized."

"You and your partner don't have lunch?"

"Yeah. Martin's wife makes him a sandwich. Me, I usually grab a Wendy's or a Big Mac."

"That's so bad for you. How d'you manage to keep in such good shape?"

"We have a gym at the precinct. I usually hit that before going on shift." He looked up as a server asked them what they'd like to drink.

"Just water for me, thanks," Sam said while Justin ordered an iced tea. "So, things still not good for you at work?"

Justin shook his head. "She's impossible. After re-hiring me, she's doing everything she can to get me to quit. If it wasn't for Paula, her secretary, I would, but I am looking around for something else. Trouble is, this is such a competitive business and they look for people with a lot of experience. I only have two years behind me..."

"But you're good, right?" Sam sat back when the server delivered their drinks.

"Ready to order?"

"Oh." Sam picked up his menu and scanned what looked like a hundred different dishes. "Ah..."

"I'll have the veal picatta," Justin said. "No pasta."

"I'll have the same." Sam closed the menu. "With pasta. You don't like pasta?" he asked after the server left.

"I love it, but I try not to have too much." He winked at Sam. "Gotta keep this sylph-like figure now I have a boyfriend."

Sam's face grew warm. *Boyfriend?* His hesitancy hadn't been missed by Justin.

"Sorry, too soon?"

"No...no, you just took me by surprise is all."

Justin sipped his iced tea. "I can be too impulsive at times. Sorry again if I made you feel uncomfortable."

"You didn't, and I'm...I'm being an ass. I am very flattered you think of me that way, and yes, I like it...us being boyfriends, I mean."

Justin's smile made Sam want to leap over the table and hold him and kiss him and...yes, he was hard. "Jeez, what you do to me," he muttered. "Things no one else has ever been able to do."

"And that makes me the happiest guy on earth." He covered Sam's hand with his and squeezed. "You going to come to my place tonight?"

"Wild horses wouldn't stop me. But I think I'd better rein myself in right now before I cause a scene. Your nice lady friend might bar us from coming back." He cleared his throat as the server arrived with their meals.

"Mmm, looks good. So, getting back to work," Sam said after taking a bite of the veal. "You told me you're good at what you do."

"I said that, didn't I?" Justin laughed his husky laugh that made Sam's toes curl. "Well, maybe this setback with the boss might curb my arrogance. Make me glad I have a job."

"It's only arrogance if you can't deliver the goods. I have a feeling that's not you."

They took time out of the conversation to enjoy the veal. Sam murmured with appreciation as he tasted the Alfredo sauce over the pasta. "Mmm, very good."

Justin nodded. "The veal's tender…" He gazed at Sam then said, "You've had a rough few days, haven't you?" He squeezed Sam's hand again. "How is your partner?"

"He's gonna pull through, thank God. I'm going over there after I leave you. His wife needs a break. She'll deny it, of course, but I'm gonna insist she takes a nap or puts her feet up at least."

"You're close with them, aren't you?" He was staring intently at Sam's mouth.

"Something wrong?" Sam asked.

"You have some Alfredo sauce on your lip." He grinned wickedly when Sam hastily swiped at his mouth with his napkin. "If we were on our own, I'd have reached over and licked if off."

"God, Justin…"

Justin laughed. "Sorry, you were saying about Martin..."

Sam cleared his throat. His face was warm. "Yeah. They welcomed me into their family five years ago when Martin and I became partners. Liz is a wonderful lady and they have two really cute kids. Martin yells at me, saying I spoil them, but..."

"Go on," Justin urged.

"Well, I hate to sound whiny, but...okay, I told you my folks disowned me when I came out. I heard through the grapevine that my sister had got married, had two kids, a boy and a girl, just like Martin and Liz's, only I'm not allowed to see them. Years ago, I sent some gifts at Christmas and they were sent back without even a note." Sam shrugged. "So, I took the hint and I've never bothered again. Kinda still hurts though, now and then. That's why I spoil Abe and Sara, I guess."

"That's awful." Justin's lips tightened with anger. "Well, they're the losers, far as I'm concerned. I bet the kids would love to have a wonderful uncle like you."

"Thanks."

"Welcome. What about the case you were working on? Is it over? Did you find out who killed the young boy?"

Sam nodded and finished the last of his meal. "Yes, we got the killer, but I still feel bad about the kid...for all of them really, living on the edge."

"Sam." Justin took his hand. "The way you care about others makes you the sweetest guy in all the world in my eyes."

"Well then..." Sam forced a smile to his lips. "I've done something right."

Justin returned his smile and glanced at his watch. "Time to go, I think. That was really good." He signaled for the server. "We'll take the check, please."

"I got this," Sam said. "No argument," he added when Justin opened his mouth to protest. "I invited you. Therefore it's my treat."

"Well, thank you, kind sir." Justin smiled. "I might be coerced into showering you with favors later as a means of thanking you properly."

"I'll look forward to it." Sam grinned. "I have to admit I like being your boyfriend."

"Me too." Justin winked at him as the server dropped the tab on their table. He stood suddenly. "I have to go to the men's room." He stared at Sam. "How about you?"

"Uh, oh yeah, I better do that before we leave. Let me take care of this and I'll see you there."

After paying, he wound his way through the cluster of tables. Justin was standing right inside the door, which he closed and locked after Sam came in. He plastered himself over Sam, throwing his arms around his neck and dragging him down for a kiss that had Sam's eyes rolling back in his head. He had an instant hard-on and got harder with every thrust of Justin's groin against his. Justin coasted a hand down Sam's back to cup an ass cheek and pull him in even tighter, rubbing his crotch over Sam's.

Oh my God, I'm gonna come in my pants… He gasped into Justin's mouth as his balls tightened in his briefs, but he didn't want their kiss to end. It was too glorious, this meeting of lips and tongues and teeth, and maybe they'd both have the blue balls from hell, but there was the promise of tonight… A loud knocking on the door had them stepping back from each other hurriedly with rueful looks.

Sam opened the door to a questioning male face. "Sorry, pee-shy," he muttered and shoved past the man. Justin didn't follow—instead it was a good three or four minutes before he appeared.

"Sorry, but I really did need to pee," he said as they exited the restaurant. "And it took longer because of you-know-what." Justin's eyes twinkled with mischief.

Sam laughed. "You are adorable." He gave him a quick hug. "What time tonight?"

"Seven okay?"

"Perfect. What can I bring—pizza maybe?"

"No, you got lunch. I get to feed you tonight." He squeezed Sam's arm and, God, but it was all Sam could do not to take him right there on the street.

* * * *

Liz appears happy even though she has to be exhausted, was Sam's first thought on entering the ICU room.

"He's awake," she murmured in Sam's ear, hugging him.

Sam grinned and moved to Martin's bedside. "Hey, partner."

"Hey yourself." Martin's voice was no more than a whisper.

"You look awful," Sam said, forcing himself to keep grinning.

"Thanks, ugly."

Sam took his hand and sat on the chair by the bed. "God, Martin, you scared the crap outta me. I thought you were going to die and what was I supposed to do without you?" He swiped at the tears that had sprung to his eyes as he gazed at Martin.

"Stop that, you sissy." A tear trickled down Martin's face. "You can't get rid of me that easy."

"Never want rid of you. You're my best friend…my bro."

"Yeah, and I guess you're mine." His gaze flicked to Liz, who was standing watching them with damp eyes. "That okay with you, hon? We can have a white boy in the family?"

"We already do." She stroked Sam's hair. "I'm gonna take you up on your offer and lie down on the couch for a few minutes, if that's okay."

Sam smiled up at her. "Of course."

"You still seeing the guy that makes you look like a goofball when you talk to him?" Martin asked.

Liz, who had turned away to leave them, froze. "What's this?"

Sam groaned. "Martin, what in hell are you thinking? Liz was going to take a nap, now she's gonna give me the third degree."

"You go over to the couch with her. I need to sleep anyway." He closed his eyes. "Go on, off with you."

Sam sighed and followed Liz over to where the window gave a great view of the hospital campus. They sat together and Liz looked at him expectantly.

"So, who is this, and when do we get to meet him?"

Sam chuckled. "I've known him for just over a week and I am not scaring him off by having him meet the family."

"You say it like that and he'll be a mite surprised when he does meet us." She poked his arm. "So tell me *somethin'*."

"*Okay*. His name is Justin."

"Nice name."

"Yeah. He's a designer, works for a fashion house downtown. Este-something."

"Okay, that's nice, he has a job. But what's he *look* like? Dark or blond, blue or brown?

"Jeez, Liz...oh wait, I can show you." He pulled out his phone and scrolled to the selfie then showed it to her.

She clamped a hand over her mouth to muffle her laughter. "Oh, my God, Sam. What do you look like? Now him, he's gorgeous, all those curls and that smile. Oh, my Lord. But what in hell happened to you?"

"Well, I was drunk."

"For all the world to see by the looks of you, and yet you managed to land this delicious specimen of man. How did you do it?"

"I dunno. Maybe even with me drunk, my natural charm shines through."

Liz snorted. "Amazing you can say that with a perfectly straight face. So, you met in a bar?"

"Right, the night before I had dinner with you guys, we went out celebrating, remember?"

"Mmm. Martin said you got hammered."

"What I didn't tell him was I went over to a gay bar after. I Ubered," he added, seeing the accusatory look in her eyes. "Anyway, Justin was sitting at the bar and apparently I was moxie enough in my drunken state to strike up a conversation...one I have no memory of at all."

Liz laughed. "Oh, the image you are creating, Sam. But go on."

"Yeah, he said he had fun listening to me trying to form coherent sentences. Well, next day he called me and I didn't know who the hell he was. Then he started telling me about what we'd talked about and the fact that I had kissed him and told him to call me, and he did."

"Glutton for punishment, huh?"

"Hey." Sam's cheeks warmed. "As a matter of fact, he said I kissed so good he wanted more. Christ, I can't believe I told you that and now I'm blushing like a little girl."

Liz hooted then slapped a hand over her mouth. "Shit, can't wake Martin. But that's great, Sam, and obviously you've seen him since then."

"Yeah, a few times. It's been difficult with the case Martin and I have been working."

Liz nodded. "Yeah, so sad…Martin told me he was just a kid."

"Yeah… Anyway, I had lunch with Justin today and we have a date for tonight, and that's brought you up-to-date."

"Without the *details*."

"You're not getting no details, lady. You saw me blush before. That'd be nothing compared to *detail* blushing."

They giggled together then Liz fought back a big yawn. "Oh, I think I will lie down if you don't mind."

"Of course not." He kissed her cheek. "Get forty winks at least."

"Thanks, Sam."

He picked up a magazine and went to sit by Martin.

Chapter Twelve

If he'd seen it coming, he would have been quicker to defend himself, but the blow to the back of his head caught him unawares and he went down on the ground on his hands and knees alongside his car in the hospital parking lot.

What the fuck…? The slam of a heavy boot to his ribs rolled him onto his side and he looked up at his assailants. Teenagers, by the looks of their slim bodies under baggy T-shirts. They had covered their faces below their eyes with bandanas. One of them raised his foot, intending on bringing it down on Sam's chest, but Sam wasn't so dazed that he couldn't react fast. He grabbed the guy's foot and twisted…hard. The nasty sound of cartilage tearing was followed by a howl of pain and the guy fell away, wailing.

Two more took his place, aiming kicks at Sam's head and torso, but only one landed with any force and Sam was able to heave himself to his feet and lash out with a closed fist at the nearest masked face. Whoever it was staggered back from the blow to his chin and into the guy behind him. They both went down and one of them yelped, "Let's go!"

"I can't move!" the one whose foot Sam had twisted cried out, but his buddies had already taken off, leaving him to his fate. Sam waited until his head cleared then bent down to rip off the guy's mask.

Fuck me. Sanders' nephew, Kirby grip. The kid stared up at him with a mixture of defiance and fear. "Your uncle put you up to this?" *Could Sanders be this ridiculously vindictive…and stupid?*

"He said you were going to wreck his career. We weren't going to let a faggot get away with that!"

"Well, I think you just put the last nail in the coffin of his career." Sam grabbed Kirby by the front of his T-shirt and yanked him to his feet. Kirby howled as he put weight on his ankle. "Lucky for you we're outside a hospital." He opened his car door and shoved Kirby inside, ignoring the kid's wails and name-calling. He drove around to the Emergency entrance, parked, hauled Kirby out then supported him while he hopped to the glass doors.

"Kid's got a busted ankle," he told the registration nurse. He showed her his badge. "I'm going to call his uncle to come down and take care of him."

The nurse nodded. "I'll get an orderly to bring a wheelchair."

Sam looked at Kirby's pain-filled face, wishing he could feel sorry for him. "You know, kid, you'd best ditch those so-called friends of yours. They tried to set you up in that park the other night and now they leave you to fend for yourself with a busted ankle. With friends like that, you don't need enemies."

"Fuck off."

"That I am going to do after I speak with your uncle. Being around creepy kids like you reminds me too much of everything I hated growing up." He punched in the number for the precinct. "Yeah, Detective Walker. Is Detective Sanders still there? Oh good, put him on please…

"Hey, Sanders, thought you should know your nephew and his punk friends tried to put me out of commission in the hospital parking lot as I was leaving after visiting Martin. He's doing really good, by the way, not that you care. Of course, I didn't know it was your nephew until I took off the mask he was wearing. I'm afraid I had to fight back, the result of which Kirby has a bad ankle. You should teach him not to telegraph his moves when attacking someone. Anyway, thought you might want to come visit him in Emergency. That's it." He hung up before Sanders could fill his ear with bluster.

"See you, Kirby. They'll take good care of you here."

He could have called it in, maybe he should have. He didn't owe Sanders or his nasty nephew a damned thing. But things were bad enough for Sanders as it was and Sam wasn't about to add to his burden. That wasn't his way.

He supposed he looked a bit disheveled when Justin opened his door, because his lover's eyes widened at the sight of him.

"What happened? Oh, you're hurt," he added when Sam winced as they hugged.

"Nothing that a kiss from you won't cure."

"Let me see." Justin opened Sam's shirt. "Fuck, Sam, that's some bruise. Who did this?"

"Some punks who won't try anything like it again, if they have any sense. Now where's that kiss?"

"Right here." Justin cupped Sam's face between his hands and kissed him, gently at first as if he was afraid it would hurt.

"More," Sam murmured, parting his lips, inviting Justin's tongue, which slid in, warm and sensuous, tussling with Sam's as their kiss deepened, becoming more aggressive and erotic. Despite the pain in his ribs, Sam wanted nothing more than to feel Justin wrapped in his arms, their mouths and groins pressed together in a union that made everything else inconsequential. All that mattered was now. All that he wanted was here.

"Sam," Justin breathed into his mouth. "Sam..."

He sagged in Justin's arms, all of a sudden disoriented. It was as if his legs wouldn't hold him up.

"Justin..."

"I'm here, babe. Can you make it to the couch?" Justin's voice seemed to come from far away.

"Yeah...think so..."

Justin half-carried, half-dragged Sam's big body over to the couch and helped him lie down. He wasn't sure what was wrong, but it must have had to do with the attack. Was he suffering from concussion? He didn't know much about stuff like that, but Kevin would know. *Oh, why are the people I trust so damned far away?*

He grabbed his cell and punched in Kevin's number. "Kevin?" *Shit, they're two hours ahead of us!* "Sorry to call so late," he said when his brother-in-law answered sleepily.

"Justin? What's up?"

"It's my friend, Sam. He was attacked tonight. He seemed okay when he first came over, but he suddenly collapsed. I've got him on the couch. What can I do?"

"Okay, Justin, deep breaths, stay calm. Is he conscious?"

"Yes, but he keeps closing his eyes."

"Right, don't let him fall asleep. See if you can find evidence of a blow to the head."

Justin ran his hands over Sam's short cropped hair. "Oh, yeah, there's like a big bump on the back of his head."

"Okay, ask him his name."

"What?"

"Ask him his name."

"Okay. Sam, what's your name?"

Sam opened his eyes and stared at Justin. "Huh?"

"Oh shit, I did it wrong," Justin told Kevin. "I told him his name then asked him what it was."

Kevin chuckled. "What did he say?"

"He just looked at me funny and said, huh?"

"Ask him if he knows what time it is."

"Sam, what time is it?"

"Why are you asking me all these questions?"

"To make sure you don't have a concussion. My brother-in-law's a doctor and he's on the line telling me what to do."

"Oh. Let's see, it was seven when I left the hospital, so seven forty-five maybe?"

Justin glanced at his watch. *Almost eight. Good enough.* "I think he's okay, Kevin."

"One more. Ask him how old he is."

"How old are you, Sam?"

"Thirty. How old are you?"

Justin laughed. "Twenty-five."

"He sounds okay, Justin," Kevin said. "Just don't let him fall asleep for another hour or so. Get him some aspirin, if you have it."

"I do."

"Give him a couple, let him rest, talk to him. If he shows signs of distress, call 9-1-1. Let me know how he does."

"Will do, thanks, Kev. I love you."

"Love you, too. G'night."

"Who are you saying I love you to?" Sam asked, sounding decidedly possessive.

"I told you, my brother-in-law, Kevin." He kissed Sam's forehead. "I've to give you a couple of aspirin. I'll be right back. Don't fall asleep."

"'Kay."

Justin hurried, not wanting to leave Sam alone too long. He carried the aspirin and a tumbler of water back to the couch and was glad to see Sam's eyes open and watching him.

"Here you are. Can you sit up?"

"Yeah." Sam scooched up a little and gave Justin a rueful smile. "Sorry 'bout this. Not how we thought we'd spend our time together."

"We'll have lots more time together. Right now, take these." Sam swallowed the pills and emptied the water glass. "Okay, now I'll put the TV on and we can watch a movie or something. Kevin said to keep you awake for at least an hour."

"I can think of other ways to keep me awake."

"I bet you can, but that will have to wait until we're sure you're okay." He bent to give Sam's lips a light kiss. "Got that?"

"Got it, doc."

"I'm gonna get you an ice pack for your side. Would you like something to drink? I have green tea. That actually might help you heal."

"Sounds good." Sam sat up some more. "I'm starting to feel better. Not so woozy." He grinned. "Must be your ministrations."

"Yeah well, don't get too cocky, Detective. I'm following Doctor Kevin's orders and by default so are you."

Sam groaned. "I kinda figured you for the bossy type."

"That's right." He chuckled. "But only when it's of benefit to you. Believe me, I want you all better real soon so we can get down to business."

"Business?" Sam snorted. "Never have I thought of making love to you as *business*."

Justin returned with the ice pack and sat by him on the couch. He pushed Sam's shirt open and placed the pack over the bruised area. Smiling, he took Sam's hand and kissed it gently. "Making love. That's nice."

"Better than nice." He pulled Justin down and took his lips. "Mmm. Even in my wounded state, I think I could manage."

"Later." Justin got up at the sound of the kettle whistling. "Be right back." He poured the water over the teabags in large mugs and brought one over for Sam. "Careful, it'll be hot." He went to the kitchen for his own mug. "So tell me," he said, sitting next to Sam. "What was all this about tonight? Do you know who attacked you?"

Sam sipped his tea carefully then nodded. "One of our fearless detective's nephew and his buddies. Lucky for me they were really badly organized. The blow to my head was a lucky shot 'cause everything they did after that was for shit. Even the kick to my side had no power behind it."

"Let's be grateful for that at least. You might have ended up with broken ribs instead of just a bruise. But why did they do it? What have they got against you?"

Sam sighed but explained the deal with Sanders and his homophobia. "He's got his nephew thinking the same thing, which is a shame, but there it is. Honestly, after this, I can't see a future for Sanders in the department."

"It's kinda scary when the guys who swear to serve and protect turn out to be the villains."

"But to be fair, they are in the minority," Sam said, stroking Justin's cheek. "Some people's hatred and phobias are hard to change, but there are always good people out there to counteract the bad. Sometimes it feels like a losing battle, but then we get a break and it feels worthwhile."

"How's your partner doing?"

"Real good," Sam said, glad of the change of subject. "He's a survivor, thank the gods. And a nosy parker. He wheedled it outta me that I was seeing you. He heard me on the phone with you, but worse than that he told Liz, who of course had to give me the third degree. She wants to meet you, like yesterday."

Justin laughed, that rich throaty sound that made Sam's toes curl. No doubt about it, he was up for whatever Justin had in mind. Except Justin didn't seem to have *that* in mind, or at least not so it showed. *Maybe I shouldn't push…*

He cleared his throat. "Uh, I don't think I ever said you have a really nice place." He looked around the living room, taking in the colorful wall art and subtle lighting. "I like that chest over on that wall with the brass handles. Is it mahogany?"

"Supposed to be. I got it through Amazon for about a third of the price in the high-end stores. I'm glad you like it. It's mostly veneer but there is some real wood in there too."

"You definitely have a flair for putting things together."

"I wouldn't be much of a designer if I didn't."

"True, that." He grinned at Justin. "I'm feeling kinda woozy again. Maybe a kiss will help revive me."

"Faker." But Justin moved closer and laid a kiss on Sam's lips. "Just so you know," he said when his lips left Sam's, "you are staying here tonight. No argument please. I want to make sure you don't have a relapse of any kind."

"If you insist. I don't want to start being a pain in the ass this early on in our relationship."

"Listen to me, Sam." Justin placed his hands on either side of Sam's face. "I know we've known each other for less than two weeks, but you've become very important to me and I don't want to see anything bad happen to you. I also know that you're a cop and the nature of your job puts you in jeopardy sometimes. I just want you to know that whatever I can do to keep you safe, I will do it. Don't laugh...I know you're the big and brave one out of the two of us, but I mean it, so don't think for a minute that you are somehow a pain in the ass..." His green eyes twinkled and a smile lifted the corner of his mouth. "Except when I want you to be, of course."

Sam sighed and his heart most definitely skittered against his ribs as he gazed into Justin's eyes. For the first time in longer than he could remember, he felt the warmth of another man's affection. Apart from Martin maybe, but he thought, with a wry twist to his lips, that Martin probably wouldn't want to be with Sam where he was right now…in this man's arms, with this man's lips on his and the heat of their bodies an intoxicating arousal that Sam swore he had never in all his life experienced. For sure not with Daryl or the one or two other men he'd had an intimate moment with. No, this was different. Was it love? Or was that just a foolish fancy—a longing for something he'd never had?

I love you… He wasn't going to say the words, not yet. Those three little words might spoil everything, if Justin wasn't ready to hear them. But nobody could stop him from thinking them, now could they? He'd say them at some point because he knew in his heart it was true…he was in love with Justin.

"You are so lost in thought," Justin murmured, caressing Sam's face with his fingertips. "Am I coming on too strong?"

"No, God no," Sam said at once. "Has it been only two weeks…less maybe? I feel as if I've known you longer."

"Is that good or bad?"

"Good. I feel like we're so in sync, you know? In bed we fit so well and like now when we're just talking, it's easy…no awkward moments. Martin and me, we have the same kind of rapport. I didn't think I'd ever find it with another man."

He tried without success to cover the yawn that came out of nowhere.

"You're tired." Justin kissed his cheek. "Let's go to bed." He took the ice pack off Sam's ribs and ran his hand gently over the bruise. "This time, sleeping together will mean just that."

* * * *

Sam awoke to the delicious sensation of a slick warmth enveloping his cock. He moaned and ran a hand down his torso, encountering thick curls between his legs. *Justin.* He raised the sheet and revealed twinkling eyes and a mischievous smile. Justin held the base of Sam's erection in his hand and swirled his tongue over the head, paying close attention to the slit, licking it over and over.

"You devil." Sam pulled him up until their faces were level then kissed him long and deep.

"You were already hard when I woke up," Justin said when at last they stopped to breathe. "It was poking me in the butt. So, I guess you're all better?"

Sam nodded. "Yeah. I slept good. Having you next to me all night is something I could get used to." *Oh, shit, my early morning brain is saying stuff it shouldn't…awkward much?* "Uh…"

"Me, too." Justin snuggled into Sam's body and kissed his neck. "You going to work today?"

And just like that the awkwardness was gone. "Yeah, lotta stuff going on. Reports to finish. Follow up on a couple of things. You?"

"I don't want to, but I started a project, and I'd like to complete it before she forces me out on one pretext or another."

"Silly woman. Doesn't she know what she's got in you?"

Justin chuckled. "She knows, but she thinks she can do better. She's most likely looking for a replacement even as we speak. But I don't want to talk about the bitch when I have the hunkiest detective in all the world in my bed. "*I'm* not silly…" He trailed his lips down to Sam's left nipple, licking and nipping at it while he coaxed Sam's erection back to fullness with his hand.

All right then…another hour or so won't matter.

Chapter Thirteen

Captain Hoskins was waiting for Sam when he entered the precinct later that morning. "'Morning, Sam. Come in and close the door."

"Morning, Captain." Sam sat opposite Hoskins.

"There was an incident last night in the parking lot of the Southland Hospital. It involved you and a gang of kids, one of whom was Detective Sanders' nephew. How come you didn't call it in?"

Sam sighed. "I should have, of course, but I really didn't want to add to Sanders' problems. It's the nephew that's causing more trouble for him. They were wearing masks, so I didn't know it was Kirby until I took it off him. How did you find out?"

"Hospital security sent the CCTV recordings of the incident. Those kids were lucky you didn't pull your gun on them."

"Yeah, I suppose there are worse things than a busted ankle. Sanders say how the kid's doing?"

"Not really. Sanders resigned this morning."

"Voluntarily?"

"I suggested it might be his best move under the circumstances. He didn't give me any argument." Hoskins smiled wryly. "So, how are you? Looked like you took a hit to the back of your head and a couple of kicks to your ribs."

"Bruises mostly, but no concussion." He didn't think the captain would want to hear about Justin's ministrations. "Honestly, I don't know what those kids were thinking apart from getting some revenge for Kirby's uncle. Kirby needs some psychological help in my opinion, but with Sanders as his hero, it's unlikely he'd agree to it."

"Wish I could say he'll be missed, but between you and me and no one else, he wasn't a good cop. Way too much bias, which in our line of work can go against you real quick." Hoskins paused to look beyond Sam through the glass behind him. "What would you say to partnering Mackie? Only until McCready comes back, of course. Mackie's a good man."

Sam nodded. "Yes, he is, but you better ask him before I say yes. I have no problem with him, but I've found it expedient not to try and second-guess people."

"Good idea. I'll talk to him when he gets here."

"What's going on with Dwight Rothman?" Sam asked.

"The deputy DA has the case. Once he's satisfied we have enough to put Rothman away, he'll ask for a trial date to be set. You'll be called as a witness and the arresting officer, so don't go planning any vacations."

Sam chuckled. "Damn, there goes my trip to Hawaii…again." He said it with humor but couldn't help but think it would be great if he and Justin could take a real trip, like to Hawaii or Cancun. "Anything else, Captain?"

"No, that'll do for the time being. You going to see McCready today?"

"Oh yeah. I'd most likely get hate mail if I didn't show up."

Hoskins grinned. "Well, tell him I said hi, won't you?"

"Will do, Captain."

* * * *

Martin grinned when Sam entered his room. "Hey, kids, look who's here."

Abe and Sara immediately ran to him and he knelt so he could take them into his arms.

"Unca Sam, Daddy was shotted," Sara told him solemnly after kissing his cheek several times. "Have you been shotted?"

"No, honey, I'm happy to say I have never been shotted. Your daddy's been very brave though, hasn't he?"

"Daddy's always brave," Abe said, puffing out his little chest.

"That he is." He winked at Martin. "And how is big brave daddy today?"

"Smart a— I mean smart fella. I'm doin' okay. What's new?"

"Well..." He looked at the kids, not wanting to say anything in their hearing, but they were intent on the games Liz had brought for them. "Last night after I left you, guess who was outside ready to clobber me?"

"What? I mean, who?"

"Your buddy, Kirby grip. He and three or four of his fairweather friends jumped me. Only got one real hit 'cause they snuck up on me, got me on the back of the head. Poor Kirby came out of it badly and his friends skedaddled, leaving him with me. I mean, what kind of friends would do that?"

Martin scowled. "Sanders put them up to it?"

"Don't think so. More like a vendetta against the fag cop. Sanders resigned, by the way."

"And a good riddance was said by all who knew him." Martin shook his head. "Takes all kinds, I guess."

Sam looked around as Liz breezed in, carrying a tray with cups on it. "Hi, Sam. How's Justin?"

"He's good, Liz." Sam chuckled.

"You should be askin' Sam how he is," Martin said, frowning at his wife.

"He looks fine to me, but then he always does."

"He was mugged last night outside the hospital."

"What?" Liz paused in the act of handing the kids their cups and Abe stamped his foot impatiently. "Abe! Don't you dare do that again, y'hear me? What happened, Sam?"

"Just a bunch of kids on a hate-the-cops spree," Sam told her. "No damage done, at least not to me."

Sara tugged on Sam's sleeve. "Who's Justin?"

Sam laughed and picked her up for a kiss. "He's a friend of mine. You'll like him."

"Bring him to see Daddy."

"I might do that."

"He the one makes you all goofy lookin'?" Martin asked, grinning.

"That's the one." He looked down as Abe crowded in against his legs, his game forgotten. "Why don't I take you guys to visit the garden outside? There's swings and things, and Mommy and Daddy can have time to talk about stuff."

"Yay!" Abe jumped up and down and Liz mouthed 'Thank you' as they headed for the door.

"See you later," Sam called. "Don't do anything I would."

"God forbid," Martin said, laughing.

* * * *

Justin was more than a little annoyed with Maria Esteban. Once again she'd been over-critical of some of his designs, saying they weren't imaginative enough, but this time she'd demanded he work on them until she was satisfied with the result.

"What a bitch," he muttered, glancing at his watch. He and Sam had texted earlier, Sam wanting to know what time he thought he'd be through so they could plan their evening, and Justin having to give him the bad news that he was working late.

Around seven he took a break to stretch and relieve his butt, which was aching from sitting too long. He wandered down the hall to the coffee machine. It looked as if he was the only one left on the floor. All the workplaces were in darkness, the only light apart from the kitchen and his office being Maria's.

Shit, she's hanging on till I've got something to show her…the cow.

He poured himself a cup of coffee, grabbed a leftover donut from the morning's supply and went to sit at one of the tables in the breakroom. It was eerily quiet without the sound of the sewing machines and the chatter of the seamstresses. He walked over to the television set and switched it on, changing the channel rapidly from Fox News to MSNBC. He was not in the mood for right-wing propaganda tonight.

He went back to the table and munched on the donut, which was still surprisingly fresh. Over a commentary by

Steve Kornacki he was suddenly aware of other voices…loud, angry voices coming from down the hall. He sighed. *Maria.* It seemed she was always angry at something or someone. Was she on the phone? No, there were two voices, one was a man's.

Maria's voice screeched loud enough to drown out a Boeing 747 engine at maximum thrust. *Jesus, girl, you'll have no voice in the morning…if we're lucky.* It sounded like she was totally out of control and the man, whoever it was, had stopped shouting. *Most likely he's had it with her.* Sighing, Justin took his mug over to the sink to rinse it out then turned off the TV.

After all that screaming and shouting, the silence had returned to its peculiar eeriness. He almost jumped out of his skin at the sound of a door slamming. He walked out into the hall and saw a tall man hurrying away from Maria's office door. He was surprised that there was no high-pitched Hispanic invective coming from behind the door, nor was it swung open to reveal a fuming Maria stomping into the hall.

Hmm…not like her to let it go that easily. Maybe he should go check on her, although if she started in on him he might get mad enough to storm out. At least then he could text Sam, *I'm free!* He hesitated outside her door. No sound of the heavy breathing or sobbing Maria was prone to when in a temper.

"Maria? It's Justin. Are you okay?" There was no reply so he pushed the door open and stepped inside. "Maria?"

She was lying on the floor in front of her desk. Her lifeless eyes stared up at him from a discolored and bloated face. Justin stepped back in horror. He had never seen a dead body before, but there was no doubt in his mind that Maria was gone, and by the looks of it strangled by the brightly colored scarf around her neck.

Frowning, he recognized it to be one of his designs. Should he loosen it? Was there still a chance she'd recover? He knelt by her body and gingerly untied the scarf from around her neck, but there was no responsive breath.

"Oh, my God." The guy he'd seen leaving must've killed her. Who the hell could it have been? He stood and pulled his cell out of his pocket and punched in Sam's number. He almost sobbed with relief when he heard Sam's deep voice.

"Hey, Justin. What's up?"

"Sam! Thank God you're there. It's Maria, my boss, someone's strangled her, Sam. I saw a guy leaving her office and I don't know why but I went to check on her. They'd been screaming at each other so I guess I was kinda worried…and she's dead, Sam. What should I do?"

"Okay, stay calm. I know that'll be hard but try to just keep it together until I get there, and don't touch anything."

"All right, but please hurry."

"I will, babe. I'll be there for you in a few minutes."

Sam cursed, called the precinct and asked for the officer on duty. He was directed to Captain Thomason.

"Hey, Captain, Sam Walker. Reporting a homicide. I'm on my way over to the Arlton Building downtown. Esteban Fashions. One of the employees found Maria Esteban, the owner, strangled in her office."

"The employee called you personally?"

"Yeah, he's a friend of mine."

"His name?"

"Justin Robertson."

"Okay, Sam, I'll have Detectives Jones and Harrison meet you over there along with the guys from the coroner's office. Tell your friend to be sure not to touch anything."

"I did."

"Okay. Report to me when you're done."

"Will do."

The building doors were locked when Sam got there. A lot of pounding on the glass and showing his badge eventually got him access from a sleepy-eyed security guard.

"What floor for Esteban Fashions?"

"Five. What's going on?"

"There will be more cops here in a few minutes. Let them know which floor." He sprinted for the elevator. Justin was waiting in the hall when Sam exited the elevator. He rushed into Sam's arms.

"Oh my God, Sam, I'm so glad you're here." He clung to Sam while they walked toward Maria Esteban's office. "I kept thinking the murderer might come back."

"Did he see you?"

"No, I don't think so. All I saw was the back of him as he ran from her office."

"Okay." He paused at the open door. "Stay here while I check out the scene." Justin nodded and Sam walked into the room with careful steps. He would have to wait until Jones and Harrison arrived before making a full investigation, but he could on his own ascertain that the victim was indeed dead and the cause of death if visible.

He knelt by the woman's body and felt for a pulse. There was none. From the look of the corpse's face she had been strangled by the scarf around her neck, but it wasn't pulled tight.

Strange…Uh-oh… He looked over his shoulder to where Justin stood in the doorway. "Did you touch this scarf?"

"Yes, I thought maybe if I loosened it she might be able to breathe."

Damn. He stood and looked around the office. It was obvious she had struggled. Whatever had been on top of her desk was scattered across the floor. He turned around as Al Jones and Bob Harrison entered the office.

"So what we got?" Jones asked.

"Victim is Maria Esteban, owner of Esteban Fashions," Sam told him. "She's been strangled."

"Put up quite a fight," Harrison said, eyeing the debris on the carpet.

Jones quirked an eyebrow. "And the guy in the hall?"

"Justin Robertson, employed here. He heard an argument, saw a man leaving the office and came to check on Mrs. Esteban. He found her like this and called me."

"Called you personally."

"Right. He's a friend of mine. I already told the captain that."

"Okay." Jones knelt by the body. "Strangled without a doubt, but the scarf's not tight enough to kill her."

"Uh, Justin loosened it, thinking she might start breathing again."

"So his prints are on it. Shit."

"Most likely several sets if it was manufactured here."

Jones stood as more men and women poured into the office. The coroner and forensics got to work and the detectives left them to it.

"We need a statement from your *friend,*" Jones said.

Sam bridled. "Al, there is no need to emphasize the word. Don't you do a fucking Sanders on me or I will file a complaint this time. I'm sick and tired of the bullshit that's flung around the department. Okay?"

"Take it easy, Sam." Harrison put a calming hand on his arm and threw Jones a dirty look at the same time.

"Well, I'm sure Sam knows the protocol," Jones sneered. "The witness, or perhaps suspect…we still have to determine which…is a close friend of Detective Walker's, so he can't be a part of this case."

Harrison rolled his eyes. "Al, for Pete's sake…"

"No," Sam said. "He's right, Bob. But I will sit in while you take his statement. Just to make sure it's conducted properly, Al."

"What?" Jones' face darkened.

"You heard me." He turned to Justin who was staring at him with wide eyes. "Justin, this is Detective Jones and Detective Harrison. They'd like to take an official statement from you."

"Oh, okay. We can use my office if you like."

"That'd be swell, Justin," Jones said, all smarm. "Lead the way."

Justin gave Sam a wary look and Sam smiled at him, hoping he'd feel less nervous having to deal with Jones. He hadn't figured Jones as a homophobe, but it was there. He most likely toed the department's line concerning workplace ethics, but Sam bet that when Sanders was alone with his friends it would be a whole different story.

They trooped into Justin's office and sat around his desk. Jones produced a recorder and placed it in front of Justin. "State your name for the record, please."

"Justin Robertson."

"Place and date of birth?"

"Uh, Kansas City, Kansas. October twelfth, nineteen ninety-three."

"Tell us in your own words what took place prior to you calling for police aid."

Justin told them what had prompted him to go check on Mrs. Esteban. "The sounds of her arguing with a man were so loud I could hear it in the break room over the TV. Mrs. Esteban is a very excitable woman, but this was kind of over the top even for her."

"Do you know what they were arguing about?"

"Not really. It was mostly in Spanish."

"You told Detective Walker you saw a man leave the office after the argument."

"Yes, when I stepped out of the breakroom I saw a man walking really fast away from her office toward the emergency exit."

"What did this man look like?"

"I only saw him from the back, but he was tall, over six feet I'd say, and dark-haired."

"That's when you opened the victim's office door?"

"Well, I listened outside for a bit. She'd been so loud but then so quiet, I thought I should see if she was okay. So I went in and..." Justin shuddered. "Found her on the floor."

"Did you attempt CPR?"

"No...I guess I should have, but she looked so, you know, dead. Her eyes and mouth open." He shuddered again. "I did loosen the scarf, thinking if there was a chance...but she didn't..." He stopped and put his face in his hands. "God, it's just awful..."

"Okay, son," Harrison said, turning off the recorder. "That's good for now."

"Wait." Jones glared at Harrison. "I have a couple more questions. What was your relationship like with Mrs. Esteban?"

"She was my employer."

"Did you get along with her?"

"As a matter of fact, not really, but then very few of us did. She could be, uh…"

Sam tried to catch his eye and Justin seemed to sense his warning. "She could be rude, I guess is what you'd call it."

"With everyone or just with you?"

Justin stared at Jones with surprise. "Why would you think just with me? She was rude off and on with everyone at any given time. But I don't think any of the employees would consider killing her because of it."

"All right, Mr. Robertson." Harrison interrupted again. "We'll be in touch if we have any more questions. You can go home. Thank you."

Jones didn't look happy, but Sam ignored him and gestured for Justin to follow him. "Thanks, guys. I'll check in with you tomorrow."

"I'm so glad you were there with me," Justin whispered as they walked to the elevator.

"You did good, very calm and honest."

"I think the tall one didn't like me. He acted like I had something to do with it."

"Naw, he's just a shithead. Can't help himself, I guess."

Justin snorted out a surprised laugh. "You don't like him?"

"Not my type." Sam grinned as they got in the elevator. "You want me to come back to your place?"

"Yes, please. I feel like I need a drink, but I don't want to go to a bar. I still can't believe what's happened. I know Maria was awkward…well, she was a bitch to nearly everyone, but someone hating her enough to kill her? I can't imagine something like that."

"People kill for the craziest reasons. You said she was arguing. Did it sound like a lovers' spat?"

"She's married, and not happily if what I hear from the gossip mill is correct. Paula, her secretary, told me he'd left her last week. That made her an even bigger bitch. Shit, I guess I shouldn't talk about her like that now she's…dead."

The doors opened on the garage level. "Oh, sorry," Justin said. "I should've pressed the first-floor button."

"No, I want to walk you to your car." They exited the elevator into the cavernous, dimly lit garage.

"You think he might still be around?"

"Probably not, but it pays to be careful. You said he headed for the emergency exit. Where's the door down here?"

Justin pointed to a far corner. "You can't get through it from here. It's locked on the other side."

Sam nodded. "Where's your car?"

"Over there." He pressed the remote release and the lights flashed on his Audi.

"Drive me up to the street then I'll follow you home."

They got into Justin's car and Sam took him in his arms and kissed him. Justin sighed into Sam's mouth. "I was scared, Sam…when I saw her lying there, I mean."

"That's understandable. A murder scene is not a fun place, especially when it's someone you know, like them or not. You did really good, though. I was proud of the way you handled yourself."

Justin managed a chuckle. "I'd rather it was you handling me."

"Soon as we get to your place. Speaking of which, let's go. Turn right at the end of the ramp. I'm right there."

Chapter Fourteen

Justin was subdued when they got back to his apartment. Sam took him in his arms and held him close, nuzzling his neck gently. "Can I get you something to drink?" he asked.

"Please. I only have Scotch. Do you drink it?"

"I understand it's good for the soul, so yeah. On the rocks?"

"The stronger the better," he said when Sam released him and went into the kitchen. "It's on the counter behind the cookie jar." He watched as Sam found two glasses and filled them with ice and a generous amount of scotch. He sat on a barstool and studied Sam's smooth, sure moves as he prepared their drinks.

"Were you a bartender?"

Sam smiled. "I've been many things, and yeah, I've tended bar."

"I can see it all now." Justin did a fair imitation of a leer. "You're wearing the tightest pants that showcase your beautiful butt. No shirt, so the customers can drool over your manly chest."

"What an imagination you have, young Justin."

"I'd be your customer every night just so I could stare at you and wish you were mine."

Sam put Justin's glass in front of him then leaned over the bar and kissed him on the lips. "I am yours."

Justin lifted his gaze to Sam's. "Truly?"

Sam nodded. "I think it's time I came clean and told you what I think you already know, but what we've been too nervous for one reason or another of saying to each other. I love you. Words I never thought I would say again in my life, I am saying to you, Justin."

"Oh, Sam. You have no idea how much I've wanted to tell you I love you too. Is it wrong of me to feel so happy after—"

Sam silenced him with another kiss. Not a light brushing of lips this time but deep and filled with love and longing. Justin reached over the bar, flung his arms around Sam's neck and held him there, lips pressed to his, exulting in his heart that the man he wanted more than life itself was his…really his.

"Uh, this bar…" Sam's voice was muffled his lips pressed to Justin's as they were, but they both laughed and Sam came around, lifted Justin off the bar stool and carried him into the bedroom, their drinks forgotten, other means of stimulation foremost in Justin's mind.

Feverishly, they rid each other of their clothes then hit the bed together, their arms and legs wound as tightly as they could around each other's bodies, and Justin thought he might just die of happiness on the spot.

"Sam…" He kept murmuring it over and over in his lover's ear, not quite able to believe that after such a shit-awful day his man had him wrapped up in his arms and was smothering him with kisses, his rock-hard cock pulsing hot and strong between Justin's legs. He moaned when Sam began a teasing torture with his lips and tongue, first Justin's left nipple then his right, nipping on the sensitive nubs, sending thrilling jolts straight to his balls.

He arched into Sam's hard, muscular body, relishing every lick, nibble and caress Sam laid on him. It seemed as if Sam's lips were everywhere, tracing erotic patterns over Justin's skin and helping him to forget the horrors of the day. Sam skimmed a hand down the length of Justin's body and gripped his cock at the base. Justin shuddered when Sam's warm breath ghosted over the head and he cried out in ecstasy when Sam sucked it into his mouth, his tongue swirling around the slit. Slowly, he licked up and down the rigid length before taking it all to the root with one long swallow.

Justin thought he might pass out from the overwhelming rush of sensation Sam's mouth was creating around his cock. Every tug of his lips and amazing glide of his tongue brought Justin closer and closer to the edge. He squirmed under Sam, gasping out his pleasure. Sam drew back but held Justin's erection in his hand, pumping slowly as he turned his attention to Justin's balls, taking them one by one into his mouth, sucking on them gently. Justin fisted the sheet underneath him and bit down on his lower lip in an effort to control the climax that threatened to erupt at any moment.

"Sam," he whispered on a breath. "I'm so close. I want to come with you inside me."

He didn't quite catch Sam's reply, which was muffled by the fact he was nuzzling Justin's taint. He raised Justin's left leg and pushed farther in, the tip of his tongue teasing Justin's hole. Justin groaned and raised his ass to let Sam in. Sam took advantage of the invitation, diving in to thoroughly rim Justin, licking, probing deep enough to penetrate and drive him out of his mind. Sam added a finger, finding Justin's prostate, stroking it, bringing moans and whimpers of delight from his lover.

Sam raised his head and smiled at Justin. "Love it when you make those noises. Makes me feel I'm doing it right." He reached for the lube and a condom.

"Oh, you're doin' it right all right." Justin gazed up at him through hooded eyes, his lips parted as if awaiting another kiss. "Couldn't be righter."

Once he was sheathed, Sam lubed his fingers and inserted one then two inside Justin, stretching him just enough to allow him entry. Justin swung his legs over Sam's shoulders and pulled him down into the kiss he hungered for twenty-four seven. He moaned into Sam's mouth at the first thrust from Sam's cock as it slipped past his resistance then slowly filled him with its heated girth. Justin wrapped his arms around Sam's neck and deepened their kiss, tangling his tongue with Sam's, exploring every part of his mouth. Sam was moving inside him now, long steady strokes that seared Justin's flesh with pleasure each time Sam's steel-hard erection grazed his prostate.

He was going to lose it at any moment and he clung to Sam, pressing his cock against the ridges of Sam's abdomen, relishing the hot friction between their sweat-slick bodies. He clenched his ass muscles around the base of Sam's cock, holding him tight, increasing the pressure inside him. Sam's girth seemed to expand, impossible though that might seem, but Justin had never felt so full, so completely sated.

"I'm coming, Sam!"

Same groaned out an incoherent reply as he thrust harder, deeper and Justin keened out his ecstasy, falling into a star-studded darkness as his orgasm overtook him.

"I love you, Sam…love you so much."

Sam's body tensed and shuddered in Justin's arms and a wrenching cry was torn from him as he came, burying his face in the fevered, hot skin of Justin's neck. They lay still and quiet save for their heavy breathing while their bodies calmed and Justin's brain stopped its giddy spinning.

"Wow," Sam whispered and kissed Justin's shoulder.

"I think my bones melted. I can't move."

"Well, not with me lying on top of you."

"I like it. I feel safe and protected."

"You are, and always will be."

* * * *

Sam was in a good mood when he entered the precinct the following morning…a really good mood. Last night had been fantastic, despite the underlying trauma of Justin finding his boss' dead body in her office. Justin had wanted him to stay over, but he wanted an early start on the day. As it was, the sky was beginning to clear by the time he left Justin's apartment.

In a way he was glad he didn't have to deal with the Esteban case. Jones and Harrison were welcome to it. Although Jones' attitude had been surprising, he felt sure Bob Harrison could keep him in check. Regardless, he was going to have a word with Hoskins at some point during the day.

His cell pinged and he smiled as he read the text from Liz.

Grouchy bear moving out of ICU this morning, thank the Lord. Be over there with the kids most of the day.

Sam replied. *Great. Be there too later. XX*

Hoskins called to him from his office door. "Sam, come in here, will you?"

"Sure thing, Captain."

"Sit down, Sam."

"What's up? You look serious."

"You know a Justin Robertson?"

A queasiness hit Sam's stomach as he nodded. "Yes, he's the friend I mentioned yesterday."

"He's downstairs with Jones and Harrison. Harrison asked me to let you know they brought him in for further questioning about the murder of a Maria Esteban. His employer, I believe."

"Why would they do that? He gave a very clear statement of what happened yesterday."

Hoskins nodded. "Trouble is Jones and Harrison questioned the employees when they arrived for work this morning." He looked down at the notes on his desk. "According to Paula Downs, who was Mrs. Esteban's secretary, Esteban and your friend had a…and I quote…a stinking row week or so ago. He accused her of trying to steal his designs, he called her names, threatened her, told her to go fuck herself. She fired him, but he called the next day begging her to take him back. She did, but it wasn't long before they were at odds again. The night Esteban was murdered, she and Justin Robertson were alone in the building."

"So, based on the word of one person, Justin is now a person of interest?"

"Sounds like she was privy to the rows."

Sam grimaced. "People have rows—doesn't mean it ends in murder. He told me about his relationship with Maria Esteban. He had no qualms about calling her a bitch. She gave him a rough time, and this Paula Downs, the secretary, commiserated with him, asked him not to leave. Esteban did fire him, but *she* begged *him* to come back. There was no begging on his part. He told me he had started looking around for something else. When he agreed to go back to work, she tried to fire him again. They certainly had their differences, but I will bet my life on the fact he had nothing to do with her murder."

"Strong words, Sam. I hope you're right, he obviously means a lot to you."

"He does. And what about the man, tall, dark-haired, Justin saw leave her office in a hurry?"

"We only have his word for that."

"What about CCTV cameras?"

"We'll have those checked out, of course."

"Captain, you have to help me here. Bob Harrison's an okay guy, but Jones…he already showed his bigoted side when he found out Justin and I are friends. I told him I wasn't going to stand for any bullshit from him, and maybe I shouldn't have. He might take it out on Justin. Give him a harder time than necessary."

Hoskins grimaced. "I'll make sure there won't be any heavy-handed shit from him."

"Thanks, Captain. Did he ask for an attorney? Can I see him?"

"Let's see if they're through questioning him for the moment." He picked up his phone and punched in a number. "Hey, Bob, what's the deal with Justin Robertson? Okay…right. I'm bringing Sam down to see him. Tell Jones to mind his mouth."

Sam gritted his teeth as he and Hoskins made their way down to the interview room. There was not a chance that Justin had murdered the Esteban woman. Jones and Harrison were way off base with this. *I'd know if he'd had anything to do with it. Not that I'm psychic, but there are signs if a person is guilty…little telltale signs, shiftiness, nervous tics, jumpiness…and Justin had displayed none of that. He displayed a lot of things last night.* Sam smiled at the memory. *But nothing remotely like the conscience of a murderer. Unless he is the world's greatest actor…*

Whatever, they are not going to take him away from me. Not now, not ever. Not when I've found the perfect man for me.

They had put Justin in a small ante-room next door to the interview room. Sam peered through the glass and saw him sitting at the table, his head in his hands. He looked so dejected and Sam's heart went out to him.

He turned to Harrison. "Has he asked for an attorney?"

"He said he didn't need one, because he hasn't done anything."

"I would believe him," Sam said, looking at Jones. "Save you from making a false arrest."

Jones sneered but, after a glance at Hoskins, said nothing.

"Okay if I go in, Captain?"

"Yeah, go ahead while I talk to the detectives here."

"Thanks." He opened the door and stepped inside. Justin looked at him through red-rimmed eyes then lurched to his feet and stumbled into Sam's arms.

"Oh, Sam, I prayed you'd show up. I can't believe what's happening."

"Were they rough on you, babe?" He kissed Justin's cheek and held him tight.

"That Jones creep just can't stop being an asshole, but the other one, Bob, I think, he's okay. But that's not what's scaring me, Sam. It's Paula." He eased himself back a little and stared at Sam. "What she said, I mean. They made it sound like she thinks I did it. I can't believe she'd do a thing like that. I thought she was my friend."

"They can't hold you on the word of a woman who wasn't even there. What's her story, anyway?"

Justin shrugged. "She's been Maria's secretary for years, I guess. She's always been sweet to me, never called me out when I criticized Maria for being a terrible employer."

"Is she married?"

"Was, but divorced some years back. That's about all I know. I mean, we were friendly, but we rarely socialized."

"Did she get along with Maria?"

"Yeah…kind of. They had disagreements but usually about work, scheduling, employee complaints, that kind of thing."

"Okay, I'm gonna get you out of here. Give me a few minutes." He kissed Justin lightly on the mouth. "Be right back."

He joined Hoskins, Jones and Harrison outside the room. "So, you gonna charge him or what?"

"Someone put you on the case, Walker?" Jones asked with his usual sneer.

"Nope, just askin'."

"And it's a fair question, Detective," Hoskins said. "Do you have enough to hold him?"

"Maybe."

"Maybe doesn't cut it, Jones," Sam snapped. "You have a statement from a woman which could be biased, who perhaps was in an emotional state having just been put out of a job owing to the demise of her boss, and who might want to blame someone, anyone, for such a dilemma. Did you question her motivation, perhaps?"

"What?" Jones stared at him.

"No," Harrison said. "And Sam's right. No other employee mentioned fights between the vic and Robertson."

Hoskins grunted. "Okay, that's it. Send him home. You can bring him back in if you get something more solid, but be careful. We don't want another lawsuit for harassment."

"Well, fuck," Jones muttered and stormed off.

Hoskins glared after him and Sam said, "He needs to put his prejudices aside when he's working a case. What about the guy Justin says he saw hot-footing it toward the emergency exit?"

"Nothing on the CCTV," Harrison said. "Not surprising. There are no cameras on that stairwell."

"So go unruffle Jones' feathers," Hoskins said, "and take another look at this. Maybe try taking Robertson out of the equation, see what or who is left."

Harrison nodded. "Okay, Captain. See ya, Sam."

"Later, Bob."

"Go get your friend outta here." Hoskins chuckled. "And try not to rise to Jones' ignorance. You're a good cop, Sam, and I don't want to have to suspend you for punching a fellow officer on the nose."

Sam grinned. "But you have to admit the temptation is hard to ignore."

"That it is."

* * * *

Sam put his arm around Justin's shoulders as they walked out of the precinct onto Broadway. "So, coffee, or d'you need something stronger?"

"It's a bit early for anything 'stronger', but coffee sounds good, and a sandwich maybe. I'm starving."

"Can't have that. There's a diner on the corner that actually has decent coffee." He squeezed Justin's shoulder and asked, "How d'you feel?"

"Better when I'm with you. It was just hard dealing with the shock of having two cops standing outside my door telling me I had to go with them to the precinct for more questioning. That Detective Jones made me feel really uncomfortable. He kept looking at me out of the corner of his eye like guys do when they think you can't see them. Creepy dude. I think he's a closet case."

"Oh yeah?" Sam chuckled. "He's been acting like a total homophobe ever since he realized you and I are together."

"Lots of closet cases do that. Kind of a self-defense thing." He grinned up at Sam. "Maybe he's harboring a secret crush on you."

"More likely to be you. You're young and cute."

They'd reached the diner. Fortunately, there was no wait for a table, the morning rush having long dissipated. They took a booth near the window and ordered coffee from the hovering waitress dressed in an outfit meant to represent the fifties. Her name tag said she was Rosie.

"Comin' right up!"

"So, tell me more about this Paula Downs," Sam said, putting his menu to one side.

Justin looked sad as he replied, "I thought she liked me. We've always gotten along, but when I think about it, I don't know her really. I mean, she's there taking care of things, always pleasant to me, kinda sympathetic whenever Maria got on my case, which had been a lot recently."

"Why d'you suppose that was?"

Justin shrugged. "Darned if I know. Paula said she was having marital problems, but a good employer would keep that out of the workplace. She was a very volatile woman, though."

"You ever meet the husband?"

Justin sat back as their coffees were delivered.

"Anything to eat, cuties?" Rosie asked

"I'll have the fried egg sandwich on toasted sourdough, please," Justin told her.

Sam smiled at her. "I'll have the same, and thanks for the 'cuties' remark."

"Oh, you two are a sight for sore eyes," she cooed, "after some of the grumps we've had this morning." With that, she waltzed off.

Sam chuckled. "I told you, you're cute."

"You are, too. Big and cute." Justin leered at him across the table.

"Don't start that," Sam said, mock-serious. "You didn't answer about the husband."

"Oh right. No, never met him. I don't think he ever came to see Maria, even."

"So, even if you got a good look at the man leaving her office, if it had been the husband, you wouldn't have recognized him."

Justin's eyes grew wide. "You think it might have been him?"

"Why not? He has motive. He's at odds with his wife. Maybe she wouldn't give him a divorce and he wants out, free to marry someone else."

"So he kills her? Wow, that sounds like a movie plot."

"A bad movie plot," Sam said with a wry twist to his lips. "Only thing is, that exact scenario has been played out a thousand times. Murder can often be caused by an overdose of passion or rage. Sometimes the murderer hasn't set out to kill, but gets goaded into it…"

Justin's eyes lit up. "Or, if he wants rid of her but is too chicken to do it himself, he hires someone to do it."

"Could be."

"Here y'are, cuties." Rose placed the sandwiches in front of them with a flourish. "Coffee refills?"

"Please," Justin said and Rosie was back in a moment brandishing the coffee pot.

"Thanks." Sam gave her another smile and she simpered before waltzing off again. He picked up his cell after she left. "Hey, Bob, you guys ever get a hold of the husband? Oh, yeah? Okay, I see…right. Yeah, thanks." He shut off his phone. "Hmm…"

Just stared at him with surprise. "I thought the creepy detective said you couldn't help in the case."

"That's why I called the non-creepy detective. Bob's not an idiot like Jones. He wants to solve the case, not grandstand about it. So anyway, hubby's out of town on business, according to his secretary."

"Which gives him an alibi, right?"

Sam nodded. "*If* he's outta town. Guess Al and Bob will find out soon enough." He took a bite of his sandwich and moaned his appreciation as the hot yolk spilled onto his tongue. "Mmm, I do like the simple things of life."

"That why you like me?" Justin asked through a mouthful of egg sandwich.

"No, I *love* you, not just like, and stop looking at me like that. You know what happens when you do that. Don't you have to go to work?"

"I don't have a job, remember?"

"Oh, right."

Justin chortled. "Goofball."

"Hey, Martin, now you, calling me names. Which reminds me, I have to go visit him. Want to come with? They moved him out of ICU this morning, so he'll be in a regular room. Want to?"

Justin nodded. "I'd like that. Then after if you'd drop me off at my apartment I'll get busy online looking for a job. At this point I'll take anything to tide me over until I can get something in the design industry."

* * * *

After checking at the nurses' station, Sam was informed that Detective McCready was in room four sixty-three. They took the elevator to the fourth floor and Sam tried to remember if he'd told Justin that Martin was black.

Not that it'd make any difference to him, surely… Then again, these days it's become such an issue again, but only among shit-heads, right? Oh well, too late now…

He knocked on the door and peeked in. "Are y'all decent?"

He was greeted with giggles from the kids and "Come on in, Sam," from Liz. He braced himself for the onslaught of Abe and Sara that never came. Both kids stopped in their tracks, staring at the stranger behind Sam. Sara pointed at him. "Who?"

"This is Justin," Sam told her. "You told me to bring him."

She nodded. "I'm Sara."

"A beautiful name for a beautiful lady," Justin said. "Can I hold you?"

Sara nodded again, this time like a little bobblehead, and Justin laughed and picked her up. "Hi, beautiful Sara."

"So this is the guy makes you all goofy?" Martin grinned. "Not bad, Sam, not bad. You're finally showing some taste."

"Justin..." Sam took his free hand. "This big mouth is Martin, my partner, the other beautiful lady is Liz, his wife, and this trying to climb up my leg is the shy guy, Abe."

"It's a pleasure to meet all of you," Justin said. "How are you feeling, Martin?"

Well, guess I didn't have to worry about a thing. Should have known he'd be just fine...

"Getting better every day." Martin beamed at Liz. "Thanks to the ministrations of my dear wife."

"That's sweet," Justin said.

Liz laughed. "That's bunk. He is forever ringing that buzzer complaining 'bout somethin' and driving the poor nurses nuts. Come sit over here with me, Justin, and tell me all about yourself. Sam can talk to Martin."

Sam rolled his eyes then winced when Abe's head collided with his crotch. "Ow. Okay, little fella..." He bent to take him in his arms. "You can sit with me and Daddy while I fill him in on all the goings on in policedom. Okay?"

"Okay." Abe snuggled against Sam's chest as he sat on the bedside chair.

"How are you, my buddy?"

"Be better when I can get outta here, but the doc said another two weeks at least, darn it."

"They're giving me Mackie for a partner while you're out now that Sanders resigned."

"Long as it's temporary. I get you back, even though you are a pain in the a" —he glanced at the top of his son's head—"you know what."

"Think he's asleep."

"Oh, okay. So what else is new?"

Sam tipped his head over to where Liz and Justin sat, obviously getting along like a house on fire. "Justin's boss was strangled in her office yesterday. He found her, which of course shook him up some. He called me instead of 9-1-1, but I took care of it on my way over to his workplace. For some reason the boss's secretary, Paula Downs, threw Justin under the bus, saying he and Maria Esteban—that's his boss—had a big fight where he threatened her. Not true. She fired him, true, but Downs says he phoned begging for his job back, not true. She begged *him* to come back then wanted to fire him again. The woman wanted to steal Justin's designs and he wasn't about to let her."

Martin was quiet for a moment or two. Then he asked, "Any other suspects?"

"I'm interested in the husband. They were having problems and Justin heard an almighty row in her office the night he was working overtime. He saw a man leave her office in a hurry but only from the back. He's never met Mr. Esteban so he wouldn't have recognized him anyway."

"Hmm. Alibi?"

"Bob Harrison says he's out of town, according to his secretary."

"Convenient."

"Right. I'm not permitted to be on the case and I know for sure Jones won't give me the time of day, but I might just do some snooping on my own time. I want to know why the Downs woman was so quick to try and implicate Justin."

* * * *

After he dropped Justin off at his apartment with a promise to stop by later, Sam headed for the precinct. He figured by this time, Jones and Harrison would have called it a day and gone off shift, and there was some information he needed from his computer. Hoskins was gone and Thomason was at his desk. He asked after Martin and the three or four detectives on duty also wanted to know how his partner was getting along, so there was a few minutes delay before Sam could get the information he wanted.

There were several Estebans with records listed in the database, but the two of most interest to him were Enrique and Maria Esteban. Place of birth—San Juan, Puerto Rico. Co-owners of Esteban Fashions—*bingo!* Maria was co-owner and operator, Enrique co-owner but also CEO of Golden Finance.

In 1997 they'd been found guilty of subjecting employees to near third-world working conditions. Inspectors called in by OSHA described the workshops as stinking sweatshops and had them closed down. The Estebans were fined one hundred and fifty thousand dollars and their license to operate a similar business suspended for five years.

Not exactly upstanding citizens.

Their home address currently listed was 8976 Briar Terrace, Beverly Hills. The photographs of the couple showed Maria, despite her sullen expression, to be fairly attractive, but the husband was stunning, with movie-star appeal. He had thick dark hair and sultry eyes and according to the stats he was six foot two.

So…tall and dark-haired…

Paula Downs had no record, but he found her on a Google search. She was a divorcee, thirty-eight years old, a native New Yorker at present living in Pasadena on El Molino Street. No available photograph.

Sam wanted to talk to Paula Downs. He wanted to know why she would morph from being 'sweet' to Justin to someone who implied he and Maria may have been at odds prior to her murder. Was she hoping the police investigation would swing toward Justin as a likely suspect? Did she know more than she'd let on?

One way to find out. Pasadena was about twenty minutes from downtown. He was going to hit rush-hour traffic but with luck he could make it there and back without too much trouble.

Chapter Fifteen

Justin sighed and pushed his chair back from his desk. He had spent the last two hours sending out his résumé to every fashion house in LA. He wondered if he'd have a better shot in New York, but he so didn't want to relocate, not when he and Sam were getting along so well. The future had looked so bright a couple of days ago, especially when Sam had said the words *I love you.* It had been like a dream come true and even Maria's death hadn't diminished the surge of happiness he'd felt at that moment.

He just wished they'd hurry up and find the killer. He didn't like the fact that one of the cops had eyed him as if it were him. And Paula... Jeez, he never would have believed she'd try to implicate him, even going so far as to say he'd threatened Maria. She knew that wasn't true, so why say it?

His cell ringing jerked him from his blue thoughts. *Jen...* With a guilty start he realized he should have called her to let her know what had been going on. Chances were that the news of the murder of some small fashion house's owner might not make it to Kansas TV, but still she'd be upset for him.

"Hi, Jen, sorry I haven't called you since I got back. How are you?"

"Fine. How're things with you?"

"Okay, I guess."

"Try not to sound so enthusiastic." She chuckled. "Oh, are things not going well with whatsisname?"

"Sam…and things are going very well, thank you. But I'm afraid my boss was murdered a couple of days ago and the police have been in my face ever since."

"Murdered? Oh my God, Justin, that's awful. Why are the police questioning you? Isn't Sam helping?"

"Oh yeah, but because of our relationship he can't be on the case. Thing is, Jen, I was there when it happened."

"What? Oh, Justin, that's terrible."

"Yeah, it was. She was strangled, Jen, and I think I saw the murderer—at least, I saw a man leave her office, but the cops seemed leery of that part of my statement."

"Why?"

"Because there was no sign of him on the CCTV recordings. There aren't cameras on the backstairs but at the main entrance there are and my description of him doesn't match anyone coming in."

"Oh, you poor guy. What an awful thing to happen. And you're out of a job?"

"Yeah. The floor we worked on is cordoned off, you know, with yellow tape. Thank God I got my laptop with me, but Esteban Fashions is closed down. I don't imagine the husband will want to keep it going, and as for Paula, well, I'd never want to work with or even see her again!"

"Oh, I thought you guys were buds."

"Not really. I mean we got along okay, but she implied to the cops that Maria and I had some kind of fight just before she was murdered."

"What?" Jen gasped. "That bitch. How could she?"

"I don't know what's behind it, but it made Sam curious, so he's checking her out."

"Oh, Justin. D'you want me to come stay with you until it's over?"

Justin smiled. It was so typical of her to believe in his innocence and to want to help. "Love you, Jen, but it'll be okay. I'd rather you, Kevin and Simon came down after this is all cleared up."

"We'll do that. Simon hasn't been to Disneyland yet. He'd love to go with his Uncle Justin."

* * * *

Sam cruised along El Molino Street in Pasadena checking for Paula Downs' address. It was a long street, stretching several blocks, lined on both sides with a mix of original family dwellings, old apartment buildings and brand-new condominiums. A lot of the older buildings had been demolished to make way for the new and the effect wasn't unpleasant. Trouble was, parking existed only on one side of the street and it was impossible to find even one space. After circling the block a couple of times, he parked in a supermarket lot and walked the two blocks back to the Downs' address.

An elderly lady with a broom eyed him with suspicion when he passed her on his way to the steps outside a small but neat white stuccoed house with large potted plants on either side of the doorway.

"She's not home," the old lady informed him. "Never is, these days. If it weren't for me those plants would be dead. Never here to water them anymore." She lowered her head and peered at him. "What do you want anyway? We have neighborhood watch, you know."

Sam smiled at her and produced his badge. "Detective Sam Walker, ma'am. I just had a few questions for Ms. Downs."

"Oh yes? About the woman she worked for, I suppose. Saw it on the television last night. Well, I don't think Paula will be drowning her sorrows over it." She let out a sharp cackle. "No love lost there, I can tell you."

It never ceased to amaze Sam just how much information neighbors were only too happy to impart to the police. He and Martin had been helped on many cases by nosy folks on either side of a suspect's house. Not that Paula Downs was a suspect per se, but here was a handy snippet of gossip.

"What d'you mean, no love lost?" he asked. "Did Ms. Downs and Mrs. Esteban not get along?"

"Hah. An understatement. She never stopped bitching about her. Not to me, but I could hear her on the phone. She always kept the windows open and I could hear every word. She was loud."

Sam was careful not to let the smile he felt show on his face, imagining the old biddy standing close to her window so she could hear without being seen.

"I think she told her man everything. Looking for sympathy, I guess."

"Isn't she divorced?"

"Her *fancy* man." She shook her head in disgust. "Well, I can't stand here gossiping all day to you, detective or no. I have work to do!" With that, she waved her broom about at imaginary dust on the sidewalk.

"Well, thank you for your time, ma'am. Most appreciated."

Interesting, he thought, as he headed back to his car, *that the old lady was only too keen to let me know Paula Downs and Mrs. Esteban aren't good friends.* A different story from the one Justin had told him that at work the two women got along okay apart from the occasional work-related disagreement. Not only that, she wouldn't exactly shed a tear over Esteban's death. It would definitely be worthwhile talking to Paula Downs. Sam glanced at his watch. There wasn't much more he could do about it until he could arrange a meeting with her without Detective Al Jones knowing about it.

Be as well heading over to Justin's and take him out for something to eat…or whatever he'd like to do.

Walking the two blocks back to his car, he thought again about how lucky he'd been to meet Justin and even luckier that Justin had called him. The fact that Sam had no recollection of their first meeting could have ended their relationship before it got started. *Amazing how fate can take a hand in things sometimes,* he mused. Maybe he'd have had an inkling that something wonderful had taken place that night. Perhaps as the day after had dragged on and his foggy brain had cleared, he would have had a vision of auburn curls and twinkling green eyes.

The selfie would have been a surprise. He chuckled as he imagined himself staring at the photograph and wondering who the heck was the hottie in the picture. Maybe then it might have begun to dawn on him, but would he have had the nerve to call him? Given his record of not wanting to start something he figured he couldn't finish, probably not.

And wouldn't that have been the ultimate tragedy of his life?

He pulled out his cell and texted Justin.

On my way over, beautiful. You ready for me?

He smiled when Justin replied immediately.

Anytime anywhere. Love you.

Love you too.

* * * *

Justin jumped when his doorbell rang. Only about ten minutes had passed since Sam had texted him. *That can't be him already, unless he's the Flash!*

He opened the door and gaped at the couple standing in front of him. "Paula? What the hell do you want?"

"That's not very nice, Justin dear." She shoved past him into his apartment. The man followed, closing the door behind him.

"What's going on?" Justin snapped. "And who's this guy?"

"This is Enrique Esteban," Paula answered with a wicked smile.

Justin gaped at the handsome man. "Maria's husband? Then you two..." His stomach dropped as realization dawned on him. "You and him. That's why you were so quick to try and throw me under the bus, to divert attention from the two of you." He glared at the tall, dark-haired man. "*You* were the one I saw leaving her office. You killed her, right?"

"That's right, Justin." Esteban grinned at him, showing perfect white teeth. "And now that you know the truth, I have to kill you, too."

Justin made a dive for the door, but Esteban was quick and caught him, an arm around his throat.

"Careful, Enrique," Paula said. "Don't be too rough. It has to look like suicide."

Justin's blood ran cold at the implication of her words and he struggled like a madman to free himself, but Esteban was not only tall, but strong. Paula produced a small handgun from her purse.

"Sit at your desk," she rasped. "You are going to write a suicide note admitting guilt, saying you are so sorry, you didn't mean to kill Maria, but she was struggling so hard you lost control and you can't live with the guilt of what you've done. Right? Get on with it."

"I'm not writing any fucking note!" Justin stared at her with contempt. "My boyfriend, Sam, is a cop and he's on this case and he already suspects you because of what you told the police about me. You think you're so smart but he's gonna bust the two of you."

"He's lying," Paula said, but she had paled. "Get this over with. We'll leave a note on his computer."

Justin knew he had to stall for time. They didn't know Sam was on his way over. He tried to work out how long Sam would be, but he didn't know where he was coming from. And what if he stopped somewhere on the way? Fuck, he couldn't think straight. Maybe he could get that gun from Paula, but maybe that jerk Esteban had one too.

God dammit! He had to take a chance. They were going to kill him one way or the other. Better he went down kicking and screaming. *That's it, scream!* He wrenched himself free, ran to the open window and yelled, "Help, call 9-1-1! Help! Murder!"

Esteban grabbed him again, but Justin kicked him on the shins and aimed a punch at his chin. It was a terrible punch, but it startled Esteban.

"Fucker," he muttered, trying to twist Justin's arm behind his back.

"Hurry up, for God's sake," Paula hissed.

Justin tried again. "Help!" he yelled. "Hel—" Esteban clamped a hand over Justin's mouth and twisted his arm. Pain shot through Justin's arm and he bit down on the hand covering his mouth…hard. Esteban howled and released Justin, who wasted no time in making for the door again.

"Enrique!" Paula screamed and fired a shot. Justin felt the heat of the bullet as it whizzed by his face, splintering the wood on the door. Justin wrenched it open and ran straight into Sam.

"Sam, oh thank God! Look out, she's got a gun!"

Sam pushed Justin behind him and pointed his Glock at Paula. It was a far more intimidating weapon than her small handgun. "Police! Drop it, bitch," he snarled.

Paula appeared shocked at this turn of events and she hesitated and looked at Esteban for help. He grabbed the gun from her and leveled it at Sam.

Sam shot him. Esteban's expression when the bullet hit him was one of almost comical surprise. Justin started to giggle until he saw the tall man slip, almost in slow motion, to the floor and lie still. Paula screamed and sank to her knees beside him, weeping hysterically.

A cop car, sirens blaring, pulled up outside Justin's apartment. Sam smiled. "I guess I wasn't the only one who heard all that hollering. Good to have nosy neighbors at times."

Justin clutched at Sam's shoulder and sagged against him, the trauma he'd just gone through hitting him hard. "Oh shit, I think I'm gonna puke."

Sam got him out of the way as the cops galloped up the steps. He showed them his badge and explained what had taken place. "Better call an ambulance," he told them. He sat with Justin while his apartment was invaded by more police, including Jones and Harrison, and paramedics who announced Esteban was alive but in shock.

After taking statements from both Sam and Justin, Harrison and a grim-faced Jones left them alone. Justin, his nausea having passed, stared bleakly at the bloodstain on his carpet.

"The landlord just replaced it two months ago. You think it'll clean up?"

"Mmm…such a light color."

"That's what I was thinking." He laid his head on Sam's shoulder. "Can we go to your place tonight?"

"I was going to suggest that. It's not pretty like yours, but—"

"As long as you're there to hold me, I don't care what it looks like."

"Oh, okay then. Pack some stuff and let's go."

In the car the events that had just taken place began to whirl in Justin's mind. Paula with a gun pointed at his head, demanding he write a suicide note. Enrique Esteban's arm around his throat, his hand clamped over Justin's mouth, the bitter taste of his blood on Justin's tongue when he'd bitten him. How bizarre—or was it banal—that he had focused on wondering whether shampoo would get Esteban's blood out of his carpet? They'd been planning to kill him and make it look like a suicide. If Sam hadn't arrived when he did, they would have succeeded and it would have been his blood on the fucking carpet. He started to laugh at the craziness of it all. His laughter took on a hysterical edge and before he knew it, he was sobbing.

"Justin!" Sam pulled over to the curb, killed the engine and pulled Justin into his arms. "It's okay, sweetheart, it's okay. I'm sorry I didn't give you more time to recover...Sh sh, my fault, it's okay, I've got you..."

"Sam, oh, Sam, I thought I was going to die, I was going to lose what I'd just found. You, Sam...you."

"But I'm here, you're here, we're together." Sam held him and crooned in his ear words that didn't make a whole heap of sense, but they were words he wanted to hear, needed to hear and please God, would never tire of hearing. He buried his wet face against Sam's neck and accepted the love he could feel in the warmth of Sam's embrace.

* * * *

When Sam got back to the precinct and before he wrote up his report on the incident at Justin's apartment, he talked with Hoskins about what had taken place.

"What really pissed me off," Sam seethed, "is not only were they ready to implicate Justin Robertson in Maria's murder, they wanted to take it one step further by killing him after he'd written a suicide note confessing to the murder of Maria Esteban."

Hoskins nodded. "So we charged Esteban with his wife's murder and the attempted murder of Justin Robertson...and this woman, Downs, with accessory to both." Hoskins leveled a long look at Sam. "You've had quite the week. I'm going to insist on you taking a couple of days off after you write up your report. You need to see a counselor? That's the second shooting in as many weeks."

"I'll be fine unless you insist. I'd like to sit in on Paula Downs' interrogation."

"Jones and Harrison have her downstairs along with the deputy D.A.," Hoskins told him. "We can watch and listen."

"That'd be good. My being in the room might put Jones off his game."

Hoskins chuckled. "Let's go."

The one-way glass provided an almost surreal scene as Sam watched Paula Downs screaming and carrying on about how Maria Esteban had tried to ruin her life and how she'd taken her revenge by having an affair with Maria's husband.

"That's all it ever was, I had no other interest in the man. He was too weak, too much of a coward to ask Maria for a divorce."

"Who's the guy in the green jacket?" Sam asked Hoskins.

"Her lawyer. He doesn't look too swift, does he?"

"My thoughts exactly." Sam also thought that Justin would have a lot to say about the puke-green jacket.

"Too weak, so he *kills* her?" Jones asked with exaggerated incredulity.

"I tried to dissuade him from going that far—"

"But a divorce would've been messy," Bob Harper, the deputy D.A. interjected. "Right? And wouldn't guarantee control of the business. With his wife out of the way, everything would go to Mr. Esteban."

"And the attempted murder of Justin Robertson," Harrison added. "Was that Mr. Esteban's idea also?"

"Oh yes," Paula replied with an obvious attempt at conviction. "He's responsible for everything. I didn't want poor Justin killed. It was Enrique's idea to stage his suicide."

"But according to Detective Walker, in his statement to Detectives Jones and Harrison, you fired a shot at Mr. Robertson," Harper said.

"The…the gun went off by accident…"

"Lying bitch," Sam muttered.

No one was buying Paula's version of what happened, in fact her lawyer looked positively sick, Sam thought. *Or maybe it's the reflection off his jacket.* After a few more questions she was charged with being an accessory to murder and attempted murder. Despite her tears and screams of her innocence she was taken to a holding cell to await time before a judge. 'Green Jacket', looking glum, followed her and the attending officer out of the room.

"What about Enrique Esteban?" Sam asked, as he and Hoskins went back upstairs.

"He was charged with murder when he regained consciousness. He'll be transferred to a prison hospital when he can be moved."

"Couldn't happen to a nicer guy." Sam smiled grimly. He couldn't wait to get back to his apartment, and Justin. He figured they both needed some TLC…from each other, and he was so ready to give and receive.

* * * *

"Well done, partner mine," Martin said on Sam's next visit. "Did Jones give you any credit for arresting the miscreants?"

Sam chuckled. "Are you kidding? Bob did, of course, but Jones kept muttering something about being too good for Los Angeles and he was going to ask for a transfer to Kentucky, his home state."

"And Kentucky is very welcome to him."

"Yeah, once you get back, and I wish you'd hurry up, Bob and Mackie might make a good team."

Martin grinned. "You matchmaker, you. You'll have to be patient. Another two weeks in here then a month's recuperation and physical therapy. I think I might just be ga-ga by that time. Where's your boyfriend, by the way? I thought he'd be with you, seeing he's out of work."

"He's interviewing this morning. One of the pattern makers at Esteban got herself a plum position with some big company and she recommended Justin. So, fingers crossed. By the way, he's moving in with me."

"It's not too soon? You've only known each other a few weeks."

Sam nodded. "It was always on the cards, but we hurried it up after what Justin went through with those two nutjobs. He told me he really couldn't live there anymore, so he was going to look for someplace else. I said why bother looking when he could come live with me?"

"Well, good luck. He seems like a nice guy. Liz and Sara really like him."

Sam grinned. "So there's nothing to worry about, right?"

"Indeed, my man. Once I'm home we'll have the two of you over for dinner."

"It's a date."

"Behave yourself."

They laughed together then Sam leaned over and dropped a kiss on Martin's forehead. "Hurry back, partner."

Epilogue

Three months later

"So what d'you think?"

Sam swiveled on his bar stool and gazed at Justin, who was standing in the dining area pointing at the table.

"You look terrific as always," Sam said, grinning.

"Not me—the table decorations, silly, although I thank you for the compliment."

Sam slid off the stool and sauntered toward him, pretending to give his whole attention to the table. "It looks amazing. You really have a gift for this kind of thing." He put his arms around Justin's waist and pulled him close. "I mean the table, of course, but also what you've done with this whole place. I don't want the landlord coming by. He'll put the rent up if he sees it. My bare-walled one bedroom and den apartment now looks like a palace. I guess I did the right thing hitching myself to a designer."

Justin chuckled. "It's just paint and some fabric."

"But in the hands of a master!"

Justin laughed. "You don't have to butter me up to have your way with me, you know." He pecked Sam's lips. "Just throw me on the bed and I'm ready."

"Okay." He lifted Justin into his arms.

"Wait, wait." He slapped Sam's shoulder. "First things first."

"But you said—"

"I know what I said, but we have seven people coming for Thanksgiving dinner tomorrow and I need some help here."

Sam groaned and put him down. "Okay, boss."

"For instance, we only have four dining chairs. So, we need five folding chairs, one for you and me and three chairs for the kids with those big cushion things so they can reach the table top. What are they called?"

"Darned if I know. Kiddie cushions?"

"Well, sweetheart, you are going out to a rental place to get them."

"What, now?"

"Yes, now. I want to get all this set up so we're good to go tomorrow."

"I was good to go a minute ago. What happened to 'throw me on the bed and I'm ready'?"

"That was before I realized I need those chairs."

Sam sighed. "Okay."

"There's an E-Z Rentals on the corner of Adams and Walnut. I called and they have them set aside." He looked at his watch. "You better get moving. They close in a half hour."

"Great," Sam muttered, grabbing his car keys.

"Your reward will be awesome when you return."

"Huh. Promises, promises."

Justin's laughter followed him as he ran down the steps.

I really shouldn't bitch too much, he thought, sprinting toward his car. The last few days had been stressful for Justin. He'd had to appear in court as state's witness against both Paula Downs and Enrique Esteban. He told Sam later that it had been rough seeing Paula so changed in the three months since her arrest.

'She was so haggard. I almost didn't recognize her at first when they brought her in. And Mr. Esteban, wow...he just looked daggers at her the whole time. I guess his attorney and the detectives told him she more or less blamed him for the whole thing.'

The judge had dealt swiftly with them both. Esteban had gotten life and Paula fifteen years.

'Despite everything I felt kinda sorry for her,' Justin had told Sam. *'She wrecked her life for a guy who I think was playing her.'*

The week before, Sam and Martin had been called to testify at the jury trial of Dwight Rothman, who had pleaded not guilty. His attorney, Alex Hardy, had backed off from the case and another state attorney had done such a poor job of defending Rothman that the jury had passed a guilty verdict on all charges after one hour of deliberation.

Rothman had caused a sensation when he'd started lashing out at the security guards, screaming that he had been railroaded and hadn't received a fair trial. It had taken four guards to subdue him while his attorney and people sitting near him in the courtroom scattered for fear of being laid out by one of his enormous fists.

Sam had wanted to wade in and plant one on Rothman's big chin, but he had to be content with Rothman's life sentence and his groans of humiliation when the four guards sat on him and tightened his shackles.

So, it was good that he and Justin had plenty to occupy them getting ready for their company on Thanksgiving Day. Justin's sister, Jen, and her hubby, Kevin, plus the little tyke they called Simon would be there, along with the McCready clan. He liked Justin's family and had even said yes to their invitation to spend Christmas with them. His only stipulation that they stay in a hotel.

'*You know how loud you are when we have sex,*' he'd reminded Justin. '*No way can we let Jen and Kevin hear you when you're in heat.*' He'd had to execute a few neat moves to avoid Justin's attempt to punish him for that remark. In the end he'd let him pounce on him and the result had been inevitable and proof of his claim that Justin was loud.

Justin had moved in with Sam the day after the face-off with Paula and Esteban. In fact, he'd never really left after that first night. He had gone back and try to shampoo the bloodstain out of the carpet. No matter how often he went over the same spot, the stain had refused to completely disappear.

'*It's the first thing you see when you walk into the apartment,*' he'd wailed at Sam. '*And the landlord won't replace it again until I move out. I can't live there after what happened, Sam.*'

'*So don't. Move in with me. I know we haven't even talked about the possibility, but sometimes circumstances change things. I know my place isn't a patch on yours but—*'

'*I love it here,*' Justin had exclaimed. '*It's so…you.*'

'*Don't know if that's a compliment or an insult, but feel free to make it you.*'

So now, for the very first time, Sam was hosting a Thanksgiving dinner. Well, Sam and Justin were hosting, because as Sam told Martin when he'd passed on the invitation to the McCready family, *'I wouldn't have the first clue about how to cook a turkey.'*

When he got back with the chairs, Justin had set out some snacks and a bottle of wine. "Thanks for getting those," he said. "Something less to do tomorrow."

"My pleasure, sweetheart. Mmm…" Sam leaned into the kiss Justin laid on his lips. "Marry me."

"Okay."

Sam tilted his head back to gaze into Justin's eyes. "That was easy."

Justin grinned. "I've always been easy for you."

"And I thank my lucky stars for that. Shall we tell the folks tomorrow?"

"Why not?" Justin fondled Sam's ass. "Can we have kids?"

"How many?"

"Two. A boy and a girl."

Sam chuckled. "As long as you're willing to carry them to term."

"Goofball."

"Hey, again with the names."

"And…" Justin tapped Sam on the nose. "I don't want a long engagement. You might change your mind."

"Never." He cupped the back of Justin's head and pulled him in for a longer kiss.

Justin sighed, his breath warm and sweet in Sam's mouth. "This is how it all started, you know," he said, once Sam let him breathe again. His eyes twinkled as he continued, "It was in your kiss."

Want to see more from this author? Here's a taster for you to enjoy!

Love on the Rocks

J.P. Bowie

Excerpt

Orange County, California

Detective Joe Brady stared at the man holding the gun leveled at his chest and sighed. "Bob, what're you doing? Apart from kissing your career goodbye, that is." He gestured at the guy lying on the ground between them. "You're gonna shoot me to protect this kid? So, like, everything he told me is the truth?"

"Seems like." His partner, Bob Murdoch, echoed Joe's sigh. "You just couldn't keep your nose out of it, could you? Had to go snooping around, asking questions."

"That's my job," Joe said quietly. "And yours, or it used to be."

The kid on the ground tried to struggle to his feet but went down again under Joe's well-planted foot. "Stay down," Joe growled. "You're not a part of this conversation."

"There is no conversation, Joe." Bob tightened his finger on the trigger of his Glock. "Sorry, *partner*... Get up, Martin," he snarled at the young man at his feet. "Go get the car started."

Martin jumped to his feet and stared from one cop to the other. "You're not really going to kill him, are you?"

He looked scared. *Stupid kid,* Joe thought. *How in hell do they get mixed up in this kind of shit?*

"You didn't say anything about killing a cop, Bob." Martin's voice quavered. "That's a life sentence. I don't want no part of it."

"You are a part of it!" Bob's face darkened. "Now get in the car or I'll shoot you, too. You've fucked this up royally—"

Joe saw his chance and took it. Martin's jittering had put him between Bob and himself. He planted his foot hard on Martin's ass and sent him barreling into Bob, who yelled out a curse and flung the young man away—or tried to. But Martin was holding Bob by the shoulders to prevent another collision with the ground and the two men staggered back, giving Joe enough time to wade in. He grabbed Martin by the scruff of his neck and pushed him out of the way, then rounded on his partner. Wild-eyed, Bob bounced back a few steps, his gun trained on Joe's chest.

What the fuck, he's gonna shoot anyway... He threw himself at Bob, taking him down just as his partner's gun went off.

A searing pain lanced through his body and his last thought before he blacked out was, *Who's gonna walk Barney?*

* * * *

What's that smell?

Whatever it was, it stung his nose and the back of his throat. Where in hell was he and why was he lying in total darkness in this space way too small for his six-one, hundred and ninety-pound frame?

The bumping and rattling all around him made him become aware he was in something that was moving. *The trunk of a car! Shit.* He shifted slightly and almost cried out from the pain that shot through his shoulder. *Oh, yeah…* Fucker Bob Murdoch had shot him and now where the hell was he taking him?

He figured Bob and that creepy kid, Martin, hadn't wanted to leave him out in the open in that parking lot off El Toro Boulevard. He bet they were going to dump him in some bushes where he wouldn't be found for some time.

They must think I'm dead or they'd have tied me up. The way the car was rocking and rolling made him think they had to be going over some pretty rough terrain. *Where in hell can this be? Down on the coast maybe? But most of the beach areas, Laguna or Newport, were pretty much landscaped and manicured…so where?* The car came to a grinding halt, like it had run into something. The engine was cut off, doors opened and slammed, then the sound of voices only feet away.

"This should do." Bob's growl was unmistakable. "No one'll find him here for a long time… Maybe never."

The trunk was flung open and Martin, his voice quivering, mumbled, "Oh, my God, I still can't believe you killed him. How're you gonna explain this when he doesn't show up at the precinct?"

"I already told you I don't have to explain anything. We weren't scheduled for duty tonight. If I hadn't figured out he was on to you and followed him, he'd still be alive. Goddamn idiot had to stick his nose where he shouldn't."

"It wasn't my fault," Martin whined.

"No? Next time don't go offering blow to a cop. Not that there'll be a next time."

"Right. I'll be more careful."

Bob's chuckle was anything but humor-filled. "Right. Okay. Let's get him outta there, and don't drop him."

Joe knew it was going to hurt like hell when they started to haul him out of the trunk, and it did. It took all his strength of will not to groan as he was clumsily manhandled out of the trunk then dropped onto the hard ground.

"Fuck! I told you not to let him go."

"He's heavy!"

"Come on. We'll just drag him to the edge and roll him over."

Christ…what are they doing? Again, it took all his willpower not to start struggling. He knew, what with the way his shoulder felt and the blood he'd already lost, he was no match for a man carrying a gun. Bob would just shoot him again, most likely in the head this time. If they were throwing him in the ocean, he might just have a better chance at survival. Survival and the soul-satisfying knowledge that he could still put this dirty cop away.

"It's so dark," Martin whispered.

Good. Makes it less likely they'll notice I'm not dead…yet. Depends on where they're throwing me.

"Okay," Bob grunted. "That's far enough. Roll him over the edge."

Instinctively, Joe tensed for the drop, however long it might be. It wasn't far and it wasn't water. The impact of his head and body hitting rocks jarred every bone inside him. As he lay there in exquisite pain, the sound of a gunshot nearby reverberated through the night air. Small rocks and stones fell all around him, a heavy object landed on the ground next to him, then just before the darkness took him he was dimly aware of something thudding against his body.

* * * *

"Champ! Here, boy, come back, don't want you running way into those rocks." Riley Peterson knew there was no need for the extra words. The golden retriever running ahead of him slowed at the sound of his voice, then, tail wagging, stood patiently waiting for him to catch up.

"Good boy." Riley knelt and rubbed the dog's ears, laughing as a very wet tongue scoured his face. "Cut it out. I know where that tongue's been!" Still laughing, he let Champ knock him over and the two wrestled on the sand. "Okay, okay, that's enough." He managed to stand, pulled a rubber ball from his shorts pocket and threw it toward the water.

He sat and watched while Champ gamboled in the waves, tossing and chasing the ball and having the time of his life. Riley smiled and curled his arms around his knees, loving the warmth of the sun on his face and bare shoulders. Moving to Laguna had been the best decision he'd made after Miles had left him, along with a note.

Met someone else, take care of yourself and Champ. He never liked me anyway. Miles.

He'd taken his clothes and personal belongings while Riley was at work and had never come back to the apartment they'd shared for two years. Riley never had found out who the 'someone else' was, though a mutual friend had told him he thought it was a guy Miles had met at a real estate sales convention in Portland.

Whatever—he hadn't heard another word from the rat, and after a year on his own he decided he liked it better that way. He'd made some new friends and the two or three in L.A. who still cared came to visit him in Laguna once in a while. All in all, life was good. If only he hadn't made some of those stupid, too-easy-to-make mistakes— like letting Miles Harper into his life. The last few months they'd been together had been their own private little hell as far as Riley was concerned.

Miles had always been a control freak, which in the beginning hadn't bothered Riley that much. He knew that sometimes he had trouble making decisions—silly ones really, like what to order in a restaurant when they went out for dinner, or what kind of wine to have. Miles would hiss with impatience, temper flaring to the surface, and *tell* him what he was going to have. A year and a half into their relationship that had gotten older than old, but his protests had been met with eye-rolls and disdain, sometimes even in front of their friends. Nevertheless, the sting of rejection had lingered long after Miles' departure, that and the determination not to be so easily fooled again. Really, wasn't life simpler on his own?

Okay, enough of that. He stood and swiped the sand off his bottom, took a long swig from his water bottle then called out to Champ, "Let's go, boy!" Champ ran toward him, ball grasped in his mouth, which he dutifully dropped at Riley's feet. "Think you've tired yourself out? Let's go home."

They set off toward the steep steps that led to the clifftop when, without warning, Champ veered away, running at a large group of rocks cordoned off and displaying a sign saying *Keep Out. Dangerous Rock Slide Area.*

He must have seen a rabbit or a squirrel. The parkland at the top of the cliffs teemed with the little critters and they'd often find their way down onto the beach.

Champ had disappeared and Riley sighed with impatience. "Champ!" The dog whined and barked. *What the hell?* He ran to the rocks and climbed over the makeshift rope fence. "Champ, what is it, boy?" He squeezed between two of the larger rocks, and froze. *"Jesus..."*

There were two bodies, both men, one lying on his back, the other face down. As a paramedic, Riley was used to seeing bodies—some dead, some unconscious—and from the looks of things, the younger of the two was most definitely dead. The back of his head was gone, and despite the fresh salty air, the smell of death permeated the narrow space.

He knelt by the other man and felt his neck for a pulse. It was there, but weak. *How long has he been lying there?* He pulled his cell phone from his shorts and punched in the number for his field station. "Hey, Val," he said as soon as the operator answered, "Riley. I'm on the beach near the steps that lead up to Cliffside Drive. There're two guys here, one dead, one badly injured." He eased the unconscious man's jacket away from his chest. "It appears as if he's been shot just under his right shoulder. Lost a lot of blood by the looks of it. Need a team here right away."

"I'm on it. We'll have the guys there in a few."

"Thanks." He shut his phone off and slipped it back into his shorts pocket. He touched the man's bruised face gently. "Hey, buddy, can you hear me?"

The man groaned. His eyes fluttered open and Riley's breath hitched in his chest. Pale gray eyes gazed at him from under thick, dark eyelashes.

"Am I dead?" His voice was thick and croaky.

"Not yet." Riley popped the top of his water bottle and held it to the man's cracked lips. "You're super-dehydrated. Sip a little of this. Not too much at first—that's good..." He opened the man's jacket further and felt around for any other injuries. "You know what happened?"

"I was shot, then I think they must've thrown me over a cliff or somethin'. Jeez, I hurt all over."

"I bet. Don't try to move. The medics are on their way. Who's the other guy?"

"Other guy?" He moved his head just enough to take a look. "Son-of-a-bitch. That's one of them. What are you doing?" he asked as Riley unbuttoned his shirt.

"Checking for injuries." He couldn't help but notice how fit the guy was. He pressed with care on the sides of the man's muscular torso. *Wow… And that is totally inappropriate, Riley, get a grip,* he berated himself with a mental slap. "Sorry," he said when the man winced, "but fortunately it looks like just some massive bruising. I don't feel any broken ribs." He ran his hands over the man's legs. "Nothing broken there, either, by the looks of it."

"Feels like every fucking thing is broken."

"Have some more water." He waited until the man had sipped some more then asked, "What's your name?"

"Brady, Joe… I'm a detective. The other guy's Martin Boyd. Is he dead?"

"Yes. A friend of yours?"

"No way. Drug runner. I was arresting him when this happened." He squinted up at Riley. "You're kinda cute. All that blond hair. I thought you were an angel. What's your name?"

Riley chuckled. "Riley Peterson. I'm a medic, and this here's Champ. He found you."

"Thanks, Champ."

Joe closed his eyes. His head throbbed, every part of him feeling as if he'd been run over by a Mach truck, and had he really just told this guy he was cute and babbled on about him looking like an angel? *Jesus Christ, I must be delirious.* Better, though, than the dream, or hallucination maybe, he'd had about his father yelling at him, calling him useless and a disgrace.

He tried to force that memory out of his mind. "I have a dog too," he said, gazing at the medic's very attractive face. "Barney."

"Nice name."

"Yeah, but I'm worried about him not getting out."

"Oh, is there someone I can call who can let him out?"

"Yeah…"

A pounding noise on the nearby steps had Riley jumping to his feet. "That'll be the team. Let them help you, then we'll get you to the hospital."

"I have to call my super, let him know what happened."

Riley stood aside as the medics pushed into the narrow space between the rocks and the cliffside.

"Cops are on their way," one of them, who seemed to be in charge, said.

"He's a cop," Riley told the guy. "Detective Brady."

"You check his ID?"

"No sign of any."

"Fucker took everything after he shot me," Joe mumbled. He shuddered as a wave of nausea overtook him. He heard one of the medics say, "He's going into shock," before he passed out again.

There was no room for the gurney in the narrow space so Riley assisted in lifting the detective's body out and onto the beach, where they could get him secured and attach a morphine line to his arm. Martin Boyd's body was left among the rocks for the coroner to examine.

"Riley, you coming with?" Brett Oakley, the team leader, called to him. "The cops will need a statement from you."

"Oh, right. I have to take Champ home first and get a shirt. I'll meet you at the ER."

"Okay, but make it snappy."

Yes, Mother…

Despite telling himself earlier that he'd been inappropriate ogling the detective's body while he'd been lying there in pain, Riley couldn't help but recall that Detective Joe was hot-looking. Dark brown hair, cut short, those beautiful gray eyes when he'd opened them, a full mouth…

Totally my type…and he thinks I'm cute. Of course, that could've been shock or slight delirium. People had a tendency to say weird things when they were going in and out of consciousness, but he'd bet not too many Orange County cops ran around telling other guys they were cute.

He gave himself a shake. "C'mon, Champ, home." He set off toward the steps that led to the clifftop, Champ bounding at his side.

He had to go make a statement at the hospital. Maybe he'd see the detective there. In fact, he'd make a point of it. Just to say hi, of course.

About the Author

J.P. Bowie was born in Scotland and toured British theatres in numerous musical shows including Stephen Sondheim's Company.

Emigrated to the States and worked in Las Vegas, Nevada for the magicians Siegfried and Roy as their Head of Wardrobe at the Mirage Hotel. Currently living in Henderson, Nevada.

J.P. Bowie loves to hear from readers. You can find his contact information, website details and author profile page at https://www.pride-publishing.com

Lightning Source UK Ltd.
Milton Keynes UK
UKHW010634030920
369287UK00001B/94